PE
W

D0427156

GO THERE.

OTHER TITLES AVAILABLE FROM

PERFECT WORLD

BRIAN JAMES

SCHOLASTIC INC.

NEW YORK   TORONTO   LONDON   AUCKLAND   SYDNEY

MEXICO CITY   NEW DELHI   HONG KONG   BUENOS AIRES

ISBN 0-439-67365-8

12 11 10 9 8 7 6 5 4 3 2 1   5 6 7 8 9/0

Printed in the U.S.A.   40

First PUSH paperback printing, October 2005

to my wife for making my world a better place to be

–There's something inside of me
Crying out for something else
And if someone hears this scream
Put it in a letter to me.–
–Richard Ashcroft

ACKNOWLEDGMENTS

Dan S. – For helping me through the tough times.
Jill A. – I think I understand now and I'm sorry that I didn't then.
Doggie – For (still) being my faithful cat.
Joe David Brown – For giving the world Paper Moon.
Skye – For sharing memories and helping me remember my own.
Elliot Smith – Whose death saddens me and whose music helped me through this novel.
Rika – For the one simple act of wearing a dress for her mother in the third season of Digimon.
Mom – For always doing the best you could.
David, Jean, and Craig – Thanks for believing in me.

All the houses sit where they landed. Dropped from the sky in pretty perfect rows of pretty perfect houses. Each and every one of them the same but with different colors. This one blue. That one white.

I run past them so fast my sneakers never touch the ground . . never touch the puddles that fill in the spaces on the sidewalk as the rain comes down faster than I can run. Washing away the color of everything. Falling like those houses fell so long ago that no one remembers that they don't belong here . . that they weren't always here just the way they are now.

I don't belong here either . . with the houses all made in the same shapes . . each and every one of them filled with stories and sad eyes like mine. Each of them with towering

1

maple trees to soak up the rain and even the sun so that the people inside forget there is a world outside that doesn't belong to them.

Three bedrooms each. A living room. A dining room that like ours is used mostly for holding piles of laundry that will never be folded or pressed or put away in drawers.

I don't think I belong with these pretty perfect houses on their curving streets named after famous dead people because I am not pretty or perfect. I am only me. Lacie Joanna Johnson. I'm not anyone else and never will be. Everyone pretends they are someone else. Everyone tells me I can be anything I want to be but I know that's not true. I can never not be me.

That's how I know I don't belong here . . that I belong up there . . up where it is that all those houses fell from . . up where the stars are drawn in like pencil marks on the sky.

I wouldn't have to run to get there. It would be easier than running. It would be as easy as closing my eyes and never opening them again. It's as easy as a wish . . *If I die before I wake I hope I don't come back the same* . . wishing every night but I know wishes don't come true. I know that because I'm not as little and dumb as my brother who still wishes on candles and pennies he throws into fountains at the mall. I know those pennies only rust in there.

I run under the power lines above my head and wonder when the rain will seep through the rubber and onto the wires . . sending electricity sparks through the streetlamps like fireworks as I run under them with my socks wet through my sneakers. All the faces pressed up in their windows to watch me running. Rain rolling down their reflections and rain running down my face and maybe then I would smile for them and they wouldn't smile back because they might be scared to see me running in the electric rain.

Only that never happens.

Nothing ever happens on our pretty perfect streets that isn't planned. That isn't careful and safe like seat belts and bicycle helmets. Or if it does you never hear about it. You keep it secret. Keep it tucked away in one of those houses. Keep it tucked away inside you . . in your stomach until it hurts so much that you have to get it out and the only way to do that is to run through the rain so fast that your sneakers never seem to touch the ground. Run until your hair is soaking wet . . so wet that my tight curls have gone straight and my t-shirt sticks to my shoulders. Run until you forget enough about what hurts inside so that you don't scream and scream and scream and lose your mind . . until you can go back into your house and smile and pretend nothing ever happened.

That is being good. That is not giving my mother a hard time. So I run with the thunder in my hair . . with the water in my pockets and on my face to hide any tears.

My mother is only trying her best. My mother is only trying and I don't blame her for that. *—Trying to keep the house—* she says. *—Trying to keep the lights on.—* But sometimes it is better in the dark. I don't think she knows that. Sometimes it is easier when you can't see your hands or your arms. Sometimes it's easier when you don't try. Because it's too hard to talk when you are trying . . too hard to say what you feel inside.

So I never say anything that doesn't sound like the right thing to say. I never say things about my father the way she doesn't want me to say them. Nothing about the way the light made me dizzy on the bathroom tile when I found him like that. Nothing about the stains that aren't there but that I see every time I'm in the shower. Nothing that might hurt to say out loud.

4

Keeping my eyes closed is easier than talking. Keeping my fingers in my mouth to shut the words in anytime I think about them because that is what I am supposed to do. That's easier. Pretending is easier. Pretending is what everyone wants from you.

That is what it means to live in a pretty perfect house even if it is only pretty on the outside.

But I don't belong with them and I don't know if I can be silent forever. The bottom of my feet hurt and I cannot run the whole way up to the stars.

But maybe just one more day.

One day and the next and maybe I can make it work the way everyone wants it to work. If I just let the rain make it easier. If I just wear the right shoes to run in. Maybe then I can keep it all inside like a secret. Maybe then they will believe me when I pretend I'm not Lacie Joanna Johnson . . when I pretend to be somebody perfect and happy instead.

day 1

The television stays on long after either of us have stopped paying attention to what is being said. One show changes into the next and then the next and I'm not even sure which are commercials and which are the shows because they've all grown to look alike and I haven't been watching carefully enough. I've been thinking about the dead cats instead of thinking about who is in love with who on the television shows.

It's been exactly six cats and three kittens that they've found this month. All dead the same way. Hung upside down in trees. Their pictures in the paper. Printed in black and white so you don't see the places where they were shot with bb guns.

My dad's picture was in the paper when he died. But they didn't show him hung in a tree. They didn't show him bleeding in the bathtub either. They showed him in a suit and tie instead. Showed him looking happy and clean and said nice things about him and I wonder why it's different for cats? Why don't they show the cats like they do with people when they die? A nice picture with nice things said about them.

–*Who do you think is doing it?*– and I'm not even sure I'm talking out loud until Jenna looks at me. Her arms crossed in front of her stomach and her eyes blank like the television . . blue like the light from the television when the rest of the house is dark.

–*Doing what?*– she says to me and I forget that we haven't been talking about anything and that I've only been thinking about the cats. That's because Jenna doesn't like to talk about them. She thinks it's gross. She's like everyone else around here the way she wants to forget it happened right after it is mentioned.

–*The cats. Who do you think it is?*– I ask her again.

–*Why? Who cares!*–

–Nothing. Nevermind.– It doesn't matter really. I just wonder that's all. I have to keep my wondering to myself though. That's why I put my fingers up to my mouth to keep from saying anything else about it. I shouldn't. I don't even have a cat so I shouldn't think about it so much. My mother keeps telling me I think about things too much. Her and Jenna both. That's why we have the television. That's why it's on. Because it's better to watch it than to think.

Jenna thinks I'm weird sometimes. I know it by the way she ignores me after I say something she doesn't like. Like now. The way she is watching the tv like it's the most interesting thing in the world when it's just a commercial. She didn't used to. Not when we were best friends in 4th grade and 5th grade and 7th grade too. Then she didn't care about what everyone at school thought was cool. Or maybe she did but at least we thought the same thing. It's not so simple in 9th grade.

There are rules for everything in 9th grade. Rules for what to say. Rules for what to wear. Rules for who to talk to and who to hate. Rules that if you don't follow them you get made fun of. And it's your friends' job to make sure you follow those rules.

That's what Jenna does. Tries to make sure I follow the rules. Always telling me when I do something wrong or wear something wrong. *–Don't be gay–* she tells me and that means that I've done something that isn't cool and I think maybe she is secretly keeping count of how many times she has to say it because maybe there is a rule of how many times you can help your friends before you have to let them go. Before you have to make them one of the kids everyone makes fun of.

I can hear my little brother playing upstairs in his room. The sound of his feet through the ceiling. The CRASH and POW sounds he makes when he pretends his toys are fighting. When the planes blow up other planes and then smash into bases where no one ever dies for more than a day. I wonder if Jenna can hear him too or if only I can hear him because I know he is there. I wonder what she thinks if she can hear him? If she thinks about when we used to play like that or if she thinks he is *being gay*?

She sits up before I can think about it anymore. Grabbing my leg like something frightened her but I know that's just how she is when she's got an idea. Her eyes get brighter. Sky bright. The words start back in her throat and move up to her teeth.

A car drives by outside and the headlights move across the room . . crawling over the walls like electric shadows. I didn't realize that it was already getting so dark.

–*Hey when's your mom coming home?*– Jenna asks.

I look out the window. The sun has gone away . . too far behind the trees on our street or behind the houses that I can't see it anymore. I'm trying to figure it out that maybe it's 6:00pm or maybe it's later because the days are only getting just a little bit shorter but not a lot.

–*I don't know*– I say. –*I think she said 7:30 but she might have said 11:30.*– It depends on which job she is at today because I get confused sometimes. She told me. I know she did. I remember she did. I'm just not sure if she said seven or eleven because some days are different than others.

–*You're so lucky your mom is gone all the time*– Jenna says. –*I wish my mom was never home. Or my dad.*– That's when I look at my feet. It's just that word. Dad.

–*Oh*– Jenna says. She bites her lip. Holds her hand in front of her face and says –*sorry Lacie*– because she forgot and I say it's okay. It was more than a year ago and I have to pretend it doesn't hurt me anymore. I can't make everyone else act like they don't have a dad just because I don't.

–*You know what we should do?*– Jenna says and I don't know why she says it like a question . . why she acts so excited like she had a new idea because I know exactly what she is going to say. I've known all afternoon and I've waited for her to say it. I don't know why she has to pretend though. I don't know why she waited so long instead of just telling me right away but maybe that is another rule that I don't know yet.

–*You want to call him . . don't you?*– I say so that she doesn't have to. She starts nodding her head up and down and her face splits in half smiling.

I haven't seen her smile all day. And then she does. And it's like all the weird stuff that happens when we are not saying anything sitting on the couch . . all that stuff disappears and I remember why we are best friends again.

It only lasts as quick as it takes for a light to turn on and off. It only lasts that long because of him. Because of Avery. The boy she wants to call. I don't like him and I don't like that he can make Jenna smile more than I do. That if it wasn't for him she wouldn't have smiled at me just now.

So that smile doesn't count. That was for him.

–*C'mon it'll be fun*– she says and doesn't wait for me to say anything. She moves over to the end of the sofa and picks up the phone. I don't know what is supposed to be fun about it. Listening to her agree to anything he says. Listening to her laugh at things he says that aren't funny while I pretend to watch the things on tv that I never wanted to see anyway.

I can hear the phone ring on the other end.
Jenna has her fingers crossed hoping he will answer.
I have mine crossed hoping he won't.

It rings three and then four times and I start to smile but not so that she can see me. I start to think that maybe he won't answer and then Jenna and I can be best friends again. That everything will be okay if only the phone keeps ringing and ringing.

But then he answers.
Jenna smiles again.
I become invisible.

I listen to her whispers. Secrets. Things she doesn't want me to hear but wants me to know she is saying. Looking at me. Looking away. Not trying to but hearing her. *–I'm at my friend's house. Just some girl Lacie.–* And I want to cry the way she says it. The way she says my name. Like nothing.

I listen for a little while. Bored. Jenna might as well be anywhere in the world. Nothing matters to her right now except the sound of the voice on the other side of the phone. I certainly don't.

Slowly I slip off the sofa and slowly back out of the room to disappear.

*   *   *

I hear her coming up the stairs and wonder if there is a place to hide in my room because I'm afraid of what she might say. Afraid of her asking *–why did you leave?–* and having to answer. It's been maybe an hour and the whole time I haven't been able to think of an answer besides *–I don't know.–*

I do know though. I just don't know how to tell her. I don't know how to say that I'm afraid of boys the way she thinks about them. The way she dresses for them so they can see the shape of her body under her clothes. The way she talks to them . . making them go all dumb with the words they say and then she smiles because she knows they want to put their things inside her. I don't know how to tell her that thinking about that scares me even more than thinking about the dead cats hanging in trees on our street.

I know it's not supposed to. I know I'm supposed to want them to touch me. That I'm supposed to want to touch them back the way the other girls do after school when no one's parents are home and all the houses are empty.

I can't tell them or they will tease me. I have to keep it secret about being afraid. They'll think I'm weird. That I'm not normal. But it's not an easy secret to keep because that's all they want to talk about. It's all Jenna wants to talk about. Sex. Boys. And mostly I let her talk because I don't have anything to say and she can tell. I know she can tell . . that she just doesn't let me know she can because she's embarrassed by me. That's why she said that about me on the phone . . about me being –*just some girl*– instead of saying –*my very best friend.*–

17

I hear her right outside my bedroom door. I hear her hand on the doorknob and hear it squeak when it opens. I keep my head turned away. Pretending to concentrate on the picture that I am drawing of the girl that looks like me only she is a ghost and there is nothing around her except for blank space so that there is no one to look at her except me lying on my bed and staring at the piece of paper where she lives.

–*I found you*– Jenna says like she's won a game of hide-and-seek. I look up at her and smile. Make it look like I wasn't hiding. Make it look like I was waiting for her to come. I mean waiting for her like I *wanted* her to come when really I wanted her to sneak out the front door and then tomorrow I could see her like today never happened.

I smile instead. Hoping she smiles back. When she does I feel like I can breathe again.

All the hardness is gone from her eyes. The crossed arms from this afternoon . . the meanness of her mouth too. Gone. And she has the same soft blue eyes that I remember from my first day when we moved here and I started a new school . . walking into a classroom full of strangers' faces and the only thing I saw was Jenna's eyes and I knew she would be the one to talk to me.

He must have said nice things to her to make her eyes go like that again. They are usually not so soft.

–*I didn't know where you went*– she says . . which means the same thing as –*why did you leave?*– only said with the softness that is in her eyes now. And I wait for the words to come to me. Wanting to reach into my mouth and pull out the syllables that will make everything okay. Knowing I need to say whatever I say without hesitating. Knowing I have to say it like it is the truth no matter what.

–*I just wanted to check on Malky*– because I hear him in the next room and it seems like the right thing to say. The only thing to say because I'm supposed to be watching him. Then I move around to sit up on my bed and make room for Jenna to come sit next to me.

–*Little brothers are such a pain*– she says . . rolling her eyes and I can see a hundred flashes of her brother Eric in those seconds before she comes over and sits down next to me. Falling on my bed carefully. Perfectly. As if Avery can see across all the streets that separate his house from mine . . as if he is watching her at every second and so everything . . every little way she moves her hands or blinks her eyes . . has to be pretty.

She wants me to ask her. She is begging me with her eyes and with her folded hands. She wants me to ask her about Avery . . about the things he said to her. It's easier for her if I ask . . if I pretend to be interested so that she doesn't have to feel uncomfortable bragging about him. And I want to. I want to make it easier for her but it is just too hard for me so I don't say anything and without thinking about it I start to fill in the background on the page where the ghost princess stares at me begging for a story to go with her sad face that is like mine.

Jenna makes a sound with her mouth. Somewhere between a sigh and a hiss. She's not going to wait forever for me to ask her before she starts talking. But inside I know that it means more. That it means she is not going to wait for me on other things . . for me to get interested in boys before she leaves me behind to sit in my room forever.

–Avery says we should go over there tomorrow after school– Jenna says and she can't keep her voice from being higher pitched than always. She can't keep from blinking her eyes and clenching her fists like we used to do when we talked about what we were going to get for Christmas.

–Really– I say but I cannot seem to fake it enough. I can't fake everything about being scared . . scared of so

many things mixing around inside me. Scared of being alone in a house with Avery. Scared of how strong he is. Scared of his spiked hair the way a dog's hair is when it growls. Scared of him being older than me. Almost 18. Almost an adult and I haven't ever done anything besides kiss a boy on the playground once in 6th grade. Scared because he doesn't want to kiss. And scared I will have to listen or watch when they make noises on the sofa while I keep my fingers crossed and hope for it to all be over.

–He said his friend will be there.– Jenna lays down on the bed with her face looking up at the wooden beams that run above my bed. Stretching her arms over her until her fingernails just touch up against my knee and I can feel my heart go all racy inside me even before she says anything more.

–He said his friend thinks you're cute.– My stomach drops and the pencil in my hand moves faster. *–That's so great . . right?–* she says and I nod my head and flash a fast smile but then quickly pretend to be concentrating again . . concentrating so hard that I don't have time to ask about him like anyone else would. Any of our other friends like Kara or Mandy would be asking what the boy looks like . . if he's cute or not. I can hear them. *–How does know me? What did he say? Does he just think I'm cute or does he think*

21

anything else?– Asking like it is the most important thing in the world to them.

But I don't ask any of these things. I keep my mouth quiet like the girl in the picture I pretend to be concentrating on drawing.

The pencil moving fast and nervous along the paper. Scratching lines in the sky of the pages . . long wavy lines that crisscross together like the power lines in the woods behind my house. Dark black lines in tight spirals like the dark black curls in my hair that hang in front of me to hide my face when I don't want to be seen. I bite my lip to keep from saying everything I want to say. Keeping everything a secret inside me about how I don't want to go over to Avery's empty house tomorrow and about how I would rather run away forever. Run until I reach a place where the world is somehow in a different color and where things feel easy and safe and not at all like they feel here in this town that is supposed to be so perfect. Run until I can't even see behind me. Alone or maybe even with Jenna if she would come with me . . but I know she never would. I know she would never see things the way I see things and that scares me too . . scares me because I can see how different we are and that she is going to see that too someday.

–So? You're going to come . . right?– Jenna asks.

I let the paper rest in my lap. Everything in her eyes terrifies me. The way they are still soft but hungry now. I can feel my voice shake and so I swallow. My throat dry and so I lick my lips like I've always done when I'm scared. *–I have to watch my brother–* I whisper . . making it sound sad and disappointed. Making it sound so unfair that I have to.

Jenna's eyes spark like angry fireworks and I think maybe this is the last time she will believe my excuses. I feel her hand on my knee . . the skin over my ribs gets tight and my head goes all muddy like rain clouds behind my eyes and I think maybe I'm going to faint because I see her lips moving and the words coming up through her body and ready to come at me the way her eyes spark and I only hope they are not as mean as I think they are going to be.

She grabs my hand. Squeezes it. I hold my breath to keep from vomiting the way I do on the first day of school with all the nervousness in my stomach. Then her hand goes softer and her eyes get weaker and I can feel my stomach go the same way because suddenly everything is different. Suddenly it is not black behind my eyes and I can see the soft colors of the pine wood of my dresser again and I can see the light blue flowers I painted on the wallpaper too. And when Jenna reaches for my other hand I realize that she is not mad at all. Holding my hands like you hold a baby's hands and I know I've been able to put my secrets off one more day.

–It sucks you always have to watch him.– And she frowns and then smiles at me the way I see sisters smile at each other on tv. Letting me know that she knows it's not my fault I have to help out my mother so much. Not knowing that right now it is the one thing I'm most thankful for.

It's much later than 11:30pm when I hear my mother's car turn onto our street. The engine humming slowly like how a cat purrs . . nobody hunting it though . . nobody looking to hang it from the wet branches of the trees that are planted exactly four feet apart on the streets in our town. But at least those dead cats are free now. At least they don't feel anything when they are dead. It's not the same for me. I feel everything. I feel too much. I wish sometimes I felt nothing the way those ghosts feel nothing.

Everything is dark in the house. All the lights are off like in every other house on the street. Even the tv is turned off. And I count the seconds in the dark until my mother's car will pull into the driveway . . waiting for her to walk in the door and switch on the light. I will blink and rub my eyes to get used to it. One by one I will be able to make out the things in the living room. The peach carpet. The ceiling fan still turning slowly. The wood paneling that covers the wall and the photographs of me and Malky and my mom. Then I will remember how this room used to feel. Warm. Safe. The fireplace lit in the winter and the air conditioner on in the summer so that it always felt nice to curl up on the sofa.

Then I will remember the other things. The day my mother removed the photographs that my dad appeared in . . the wood paneling not as faded in those spots. Blank squares where the wood is darker. Blank squares that are like memories that make me remember that this room does not feel so safe and warm anymore . . that make me remember why I'm sitting here in the dark with all the lights off.

The sound of her car gets louder . . the headlights shine through the windows like stars landing on the ground. The light moving across the room and across my hands . . across the silent screen of the tv before shutting off.

The sound of the car engine replaced with the sound of the car door opening then closing.

My mother is late again. I saw the clock when the head-lights crawled along the room. Almost 2:00am. Later than yesterday. Later than last week too. I get worried when she's so late . . worried that one day she won't even come home. I don't tell her this though. She doesn't want to hear me tell her this. She's too tired to hear about all the things I worry about. She has her own things to worry about and I shouldn't try to make her feel worse.

I can hear her key slide into the lock like a loud cricket chirping and the key twisting back and forth until it clicks. The door creaking open. The light switching on and my mother's bags dropping to the floor and her shoes thrown off. She sighs then as she does every night. Taking a minute before she comes and turns on the light in the living room where she will be startled by me sitting in the darkness . . same as she is every night.

She doesn't scream when she sees me. Not like she used to. She only grabs her chest now . . says *—Oh god you startled me Lacie—* though I don't know why she is so startled every night. I don't know why she never expects me to be here the way I expect her every night.

—Why don't you ever turn on the lights?— she says as she sits down next to me. *—You'll ruin your eyes sitting here in the dark.—* And I don't say anything . . just let her talk so I can hear the sound of her voice . . letting her ask her ques-

27

tions like she is reading an old list that we have both memorized the answers to.

–Is Malky in bed?–
and I nod.

–Did you guys eat dinner?–
and I nod.

–Was Jenna over? Did you guys have a good time?–
and I nod.

–Did anyone call?–
and I shake my head.

My mother's shoulders sag . . her head falls back against
the pillow on the sofa and she spreads her arms and pats her
stomach. I bring my knees up on the sofa and put my head
down on her lap and let her hands run through my hair the
way I do every night. Put my fingers in my mouth the way
I've always done since I was small and close my eyes and
now the room feels a little bit safe again . . warm again.

–You're late– I mumble and my mother answers with her
hand moving a little quicker through my hair . . her finger-

nails scratching a little harder on the back of my neck. But still I can feel how light her arms are . . how tired her body is . . weightless and frail like worn paper and I wish she would never go back there. To the diner where she works at night. Or to the office where she works during the day. I wish she could stay away from those places. But I know things are more complicated than wanting and wishing and so I don't say any more.

–*I'm sorry. I meant to call but we were busy*– she tells me. Then she tells me I should have gone to bed. That I shouldn't wait up for her. But I can't sleep before she gets home. Not until I know everything is okay. –*You can't keep doing this*– she says . . says I can't keep worrying the way that I do . . that it's not good for me . . that it's not good for her because she is worried about me. And I think if she only knew everything how much more she would worry about me. I don't want her to and that is why I don't ever tell her all the things that I think about.

–*Okay Mom*– I say. I say it every night. I say it and I do really mean it only I don't know how to make it true. But it is too late in the night to think anymore. It is too late to worry about tomorrow night already so I close my eyes tighter and listen to the ticking of the clock above the fireplace. Feeling myself drift away . . floating like the ghosts of the cats that dance in the trees . . nothing around me like the girl in my drawings.

–*Lacie my baby*– my mother whispers the way she's always done . . the sound of her voice making my eyes hurt and my throat clump up. –*I promise*– she whispers and I know what she is promising. I know she is promising better things . . promising me that it won't hurt so much tomorrow as it hurts today and that every day it will hurt less. A promise that she can't keep no matter how hard she tries.

day 14

–That's him. Over there. See? Behind that girl in the blue shirt. That's him.–

I try to see where Jenna is pointing . . moving my head to where her head is and hoping to see the girl in the blue shirt first and then look behind her to see the boy who is supposed to like me. But there are too many people to see. The cafeteria tables are too crowded to notice one person from the rest.

–You see him?– Jenna whines. She is getting impatient with me but it's not my fault . . then someone moves . . then I see a blue shirt and I see two people sitting across the table from her . . one is Avery with his black hair perfectly in place and the other must be him.

–*I see him*– I say. I see him but I can't really see his face. I can only see that he is shorter than Avery. That his hair isn't dark or perfect. His eyes almost closed and quiet. The bones in his shoulders show through his shirt like the branches of a pointy tree.

–*Well?*– Jenna says to me. She wants me to fall in love with him. She's been wanting me to fall in love with him for two weeks. Trying to make me meet him. Trying anything for me to see him but always the wrong time and wrong place. Two weeks of excuses that I have made. Two weeks of me avoiding the right time and right place until I got stuck today because he wasn't even supposed to be in our lunch period. Now this is the first time I have ever seen him. I mean the first time I've seen him that he is not just walking by or that I'm not hurrying off somewhere or trying to look in the wrong direction. This is the first time I get to stare at him and already Jenna wants me to say I love him. Already she is planning things for the four of us to do. Her . . Avery . . me . . and this boy Benji . . the boy with quiet eyes . . the boy whose voice I still have never heard.

–*WELL?*–

–*Well what?*– I try to sound like I don't care . . try to sound calm but Jenna sees right through me . . sees I'm trying to avoid talking about him the same way I've done since she first brought him up that time on my bed and she rolls her eyes and tells me not to *be gay*.

I know exactly what she wants to know. If I think he's cute. If I think I could like him. If I want him to come over and talk to me. If I want to hold his hand. If I want him to put his hand under my shirt. If I want him to put his thing inside me the way she says she wants Avery to. But more than that she wants to know if I'm going to go along with her . . if I'm going to stop being shy for the first time.

I can't bring myself to say anything.

I feel her eyes on me . . crawling like ants on my face trying to get inside me . . wanting to get out what I'm feeling inside and carry it back to her so that she doesn't have to keep asking and keep getting nothing back from me. Staring at me . . her hands thrown out to her sides . . waiting for me to say something . . giving me one last chance before she gets annoyed with me. I can't take her looking at me this way. But it makes me too uncomfortable to talk so I look down at my hands playing with my food. Look there until Jenna's mouth drops open because she can't believe I'm going to stay quiet again . . too pissed at me to care anymore and she turns away.

When she looks away I can look up again. My turn to stare at her . . the back of her head with her straight brown hair brushed through that hangs so long past her shoulders . . so pretty and perfect. I touch the ends of my hair . . just above my shoulders . . tight ugly curls like a poodle. And maybe it wouldn't be so hard if I was as pretty as Jenna. Maybe then I could be into all the things she is. Wondering when it happened that I got left behind her in all these things. Last year? The year before? Sometime I guess. When my dad died maybe. Like I stopped getting older and all the other girls have changed while I've stayed the same.

It's not even just my clothes and my hair and the way they put on makeup between every class that make me feel so immature next to them. It's more than just those things. It's the way they talk with their eyes. The way they move their hands . . sophisticated . . mature.

I want to be that way too. I want it to come so easy for me the way it does for Jenna and Kara and even Mandy who is almost a whole year younger than me. I want to be that way so that I fit in.

Everything feels so slow for me . . like I'm dragging through sand and they are all shooting past like tiny sparks of electricity . . so fast that I can see bright trails behind them where they go ahead . . see them changing the way they act . . the things they like . . the stuff they talk about and I only want things to stay the same as they have always been.

It's the same way it was when I was nine and I was the only one who couldn't ride a bike . . running to keep up with my friends who would complain they had to ride slower so I could run alongside them. But they would ride a little bit faster every day and I would fall a little bit farther behind and they would wait a little bit less than they used to so that I didn't have a choice. I had to learn how to ride a bike myself or eventually I would be left standing all alone.

It's the same now. Jenna is not going to slow down anymore. She is going to pedal as fast as she can if I don't try this time. If I don't try with this boy who is sitting across the room from me . . thinking about me. If I don't try then she will leave me standing somewhere by myself . . I will be at my house by myself because Jenna will not keep coming over if I don't try.

I don't even have to try for too long. Just pretend long enough so that Jenna stops looking at me like I'm not normal . . long enough so my friends don't start saying things about me the way some of the other kids do . . a week maybe two with him and that should be okay. I can pretend for a week.

I look again for him . . looking past the girl with the blue shirt until I see him. This time I can see his face beneath the hair that hangs in front of his eyes until he pushes it away . . and he looks younger . . safer somehow than Avery with his strong features . . he looks smaller and nicer and he doesn't look so bad . . cute enough. And it doesn't matter that I'm scared or that my stomach is turning over inside me . . I have to do this.

I have to.

When he sees me looking at him I have to keep myself from looking away . . have to concentrate on keeping my eyes open . . have to try to not look scared. I have to pretend I don't care the same way I've seen Jenna do. I have to pinch my leg under the table to keep myself from looking away when he is looking at me the way an animal looks at you to see if you are shy or afraid. His eyes studying me and I can feel them looking deeper . . trying to find me where I hide.

I don't turn away.

I feel my hand tremble. I feel my skin getting bruised where my fingernails pinch so hard that I might faint.

But I don't turn away.

Then I blink my eyes and I force my lips to smile just a little bit the way I've practiced in the mirror so many times since I was little . . pretending I am smiling at a prince . . that I am a princess.

I see the color rush to his face . . making his cheeks red . . I see him trying not to smile but not being able to stop so that he brings his hand to his mouth. Not to cover it like I thought though . . only to push the hair from his face again and I want to turn away more than ever but know that I can't. Not yet. Not until he does.

I know my face has turned bright pink the way his has . . only brighter . . more obvious than his because of how pale my skin is . . because of how dark my eyes are . . my hair black and my face all pink and I must look stupid. And I know I will have to turn away any second if he doesn't because I can't breathe anymore.

When I can't take it any longer he waves . . his hand clumsy . . a short quick wave before bringing his hand back down and I feel myself do the same . . waving . . then quickly moving my hand to play with my hair again . . then people walk between us . . and when they move he is looking away.

I take a deep breath and feel Jenna's hand grab my leg under the table.

She is smiling wider than I've ever seen her smile and I know she has been watching me the whole time . . letting the plans she was dreaming about become more and more real. I don't look at her for long. I don't say anything right now either. Right now I want to say nothing. Just keep pedaling like the first time on a bike. Maybe I will be able to keep my balance. Riding along but knowing sooner or later I will fall again . . hoping that when I do I will be able to get back on.

The hallways are filled with faces passing in every direction . . lockers opening and closing . . announcements with urgent information that no one is listening to . . a million voices trying to talk over each other to figure out where and who is going to do what now that the school day is over. Jenna is one of those voices . . talking over the person who is talking next to her. I try to focus in on what she is saying.

—It would just be for a little bit— she says. *—We'll be back before your brother gets home.—*

My brother gets home at 4:30pm. My mother gets home at 7:30pm and I'm supposed to get home by 3:30pm. I'm supposed to be there when my brother comes home from his after-school program. I have to watch him . . I have to because there is no one else and nine is too young to watch

yourself. Jenna knows all of this. Jenna knows I can't do it . .
knows I have to be home . . that I can't be late. Anything
could happen between now and then to make me late even
if we do everything the way we are supposed to . . any little
thing could . . that is why I always go home right after
school. That is why I can't go and it's not even an excuse
this time . . not completely.

I shake my head.
I can't.

I can't go with her to Avery's house even if it is only for
an hour. I have to be home when Malky gets home. He will
be too scared to come home alone . . he will feel the way I
feel when my mother comes home late . . he will feel the
way I felt when my father was home dead waiting for us.

I shake my head.

–*God Lacie. You'll be home. It'll be fine.*– But my head is
full of *what ifs* and my stomach is full of butterflies and I
don't know that I'm ready. –*Avery's got his driver's license he
will drive you home in time!*– and there is another rule I'm
not allowed to break . . driving with someone my mother
doesn't know . . NO . . everything seems all wrong with
this. I don't even know Benji yet I haven't even spoken to

him yet. I don't know him at all and certainly not enough to break all these rules for him.

—Jenna I can't.— I'm begging her . . don't make me do this . .

—You can. You just don't want to!— Her voice angry . . the words slithering through her teeth . . and I know she won't go if I don't . . that no matter how much she flirts and shows off she is too scared to go there alone. That's why it's so important to her. That's why she is giving me such a hard time. I know she might hate me if I don't and I know that is why I will have to say yes sooner or later . . that she will make me say yes . . make me do what she wants same as always.

—You can just come over to my house.— Trying one last time . . trying once more to keep everything the way it has always been.

—I don't want to go to your stupid house!— she shouts . . the girl standing next to her stops talking and turns to look at us . . looks at Jenna who looks like she wants to pull my hair out . . looking at me and I can feel my face turning red again . . wanting to disappear . . to be invisible. Then the girl laughs . . whispers something and then starts talking again like nothing happened.

Jenna crosses her arms in front of her. Lets her weight shift onto one leg and taps her foot. And I know now that everything has changed between us . . that she will never come over to my house just to watch tv anymore . . that I have to go along with her right now or go away forever. And it's so confusing that it can happen just like that . . that with a few words five years can change in five minutes.

I'm trying to put things in the right places in my mind. Too many things coming in all at once like too many movies playing on the same movie screen. Malky coming home and finding the door locked and using the key under the rock in the garden that I use. What would he think if no one was home? Would he call Mom? She would lose her mind worrying about me. She has too much to worry about . . the bills . . the house . . it's not fair to make her worry about me.

But what about me? My mom says I can't hide my whole life . . that I have to stop being afraid. She says I shouldn't be so –disconnected.– So maybe I should? It would mean a lot to Jenna.

She is still standing there with her arms folded when I see Avery and Benji way down at the end of the hall. They are walking toward us. Yes or no? Jenna sees them now.

Looks at me again . . giving me another chance. *–You PROMISE we will be back on time?–* I whisper and Jenna shouts . . claps her hands once and jumps up and down . . promising the whole time.

I put my hands in my pockets . . keeping my fingers crossed so no one can see them . . hoping that everything will go alright as they walk up . . trying not to think about what is going to happen at Avery's house . . just waiting for it to all be over so I can be safe at home again.

*   *   *

The windows are all down and the wind is blowing into the backseat where I am . . the cornfields around our school go by at circus speed and I get dizzy watching the rows and rows of dried and broken stalks that were planted in neat lines back in spring. Dead now. Harvested. And I look up from looking at the rows and see the whole field . . browned and burnt like a forest plowed under by giant machines.

The fields go so far back that they are all I can see except the small farmhouse that sits in the middle . . circled by three tall trees that have started to change color. And I think about how great it would be to run through those cornstalks . . running with my arms spread out like a bird until my hands hurt so bad from banging into each one as I pass . . running until I made it to that house and how nice it must be to live in a house that is so far away from everywhere else.

If I close my eyes the right way I can pretend that I am running . . the wind on my face the right way. I can forget about the sound of the tires on the asphalt and the rattling of the engine . . I can forget about the people in the car and where we are going . . about rules that are being broken. If I close my eyes the right way I can forget about the world and everything in it and then there is only me . . running.

–I can close the window if that's too much wind– Avery says . . his voice bringing me back . . making everything real . . the way his eyes stare straight ahead where there is nothing but more road in front of him . . the way his foot is making the car go faster and faster and never slowing down. I wish he would slow down . . wish the car would stop and never start again and I could walk home from here and be

home on time if I hurried . . if I cut through the fields and came out behind the shopping center near my house.

–I'm okay– I whisper but I don't think anyone can hear me . . the wind rushing in so loud . . the radio playing under the rushing sound of the wind so I can only hear enough of it to know that it is on but not enough to hear words or songs or anything that I recognize. No one heard me whisper but that doesn't matter though because no one is paying attention to me . . Avery only asked to be polite. I can see his eyes in the rearview mirror . . staring ahead and only pausing every now and then to look at Jenna in the front seat next to him and I know that Benji is doing the same in the seat next to me even if I can't see him.

I won't look at him though . . I keep my eyes looking out the window . . watching the cornfields turn into pine trees like a slow-motion magic trick.

Those trees grow thin after a few more miles . . a few more minutes . . becoming fences and houses as the road curves around them . . curving so much for so long that the road is not empty in front of us anymore . . traffic lights and stop signs and cars waiting their turn to go here and there and my stomach gets a little more nervous now that we slow

47

down because that means we are getting closer to where we are going.

I have to think about it now. Avery's house with the empty rooms . . no parents home . . nothing to stop us from doing things we are not supposed to . . things I'm afraid of doing. I don't know that I'm brave enough to stop them from happening. I don't know if it's harder to admit being afraid or to just do those things anyway.

I don't know if I could say no . . all the silence in the rooms . . them watching me . . Jenna watching me and wanting me to do them . . no sounds of cars or of the wind blowing in through the window to hide in. Nowhere to look away. Nothing to keep me safe.

The car slows down . . stops as a traffic light turns from yellow to red.

Jenna pops her head around . . leaning between the front seats to look at me. She flashes a quick smile . . winks . . then turns back around and I know she is as nervous as I am . . but excited nervous. I know she is because she isn't saying anything . . because she isn't chatting the way she always does and has become as quiet as me.

I keep my fingers crossed as the car starts to go again . . passing over the road that goes to my house if we turned right . . but going straight into the development where Avery lives. The houses in pretty perfect rows like in my neighborhood . . yellow and white and the next one blue and I watch the reflection of the car off the empty windows of each house . . wondering which might be his . . trying to guess . . the next one . . maybe two more . . but the car isn't slowing down . . then a little at a time his foot switches from the gas pedal to the brake and the houses go by not quite so fast. The car turns all of a sudden . . parking in the driveway of a white house with white brick and white aluminum siding . . his fingers turning the keys and all of a sudden the radio stops . . all of a sudden there is no sound at all except the birds flying south above our heads and I have to remember to breathe when surrounded by so much silence.

–Last stop– Avery says and Jenna laughs. It is a fake laugh. It is part of the way she acts around him . . the way she's been acting since they came up to us in the hallway and I'm realizing that I don't like her so much acting this way . . acting dumb.

I have to wait for her to get out of the car and pull the front seat up so that I can climb out . . ducking my head

49

and pulling my arms in close and getting out of the car is like a complicated gymnastics move that I never noticed until now when I feel all three of them watching me. I feel like I'm almost going to fall . . to trip on the seat belt and land in the driveway while they watch . . I don't . . I look down at my feet to keep my balance . . looking down at my feet to keep from letting them see me where my face has gone all red . . looking at my watch and thinking only 45 minutes more.

*   *   *

He does it without even trying . . his hand moving like he has memorized the places of her buttons all those times he looked over at her instead of looking where he was driving. I'm watching the way his fingers slip through the tiny spaces . . the buttons sliding open and one by one Jenna's shirt opens . . falling apart down the middle from her neck until I see her belly button and she softly throws her head back to let Avery's hands move underneath and onto her sides.

I try to look away but I don't want to look at Benji who Avery has been calling *Dogboy* since we've gotten here. I don't want to look at him . . I don't want to see his eyes looking at me . . wanting me the way Jenna is with her mouth open just a little and her spine bent just a little . . wanting to put his teeth on me the way Avery puts his teeth on Jenna's neck. I don't want to see his eyes and learn that they call him Dogboy because he wants to bite me . . that he's meaner than the puppy he resembles with his soft hair and soft eyes . . looking at me like I am one of those cats that hangs from the trees and he wants to be the one that splits me open for them to take pictures of for the newspapers.

Avery's hands move so slow like he's practiced a million times . . moving up from her waist and over her breasts then quickly back down.

I think about how I would have kept them there longer like when I'm alone in my room at night . . my hands moving along my ribs . . but those are my hands and not a stranger's and I wonder how long I would want a stranger to leave his hands there . . probably not long . . probably not ever . . I wonder how Jenna must feel and wonder if Avery can feel her heart beating under her skin the way mine is from watching them.

When he moves his face to hers I see her open her mouth more and I see her tongue come out just a little and I wonder how she knows how to do everything the way she is supposed to . . wondering if I would know what to do if it were me. Because that scares me almost as much as doing it . . the not knowing how to.

I watch them kissing. I watch her put her hands around his neck . . her eyes closed so she doesn't know that I am watching but I don't know that she cares. Maybe she wants me to watch them. I keep watching them . . thinking about Benji watching me . . knowing he is pretending it is me and him.

I don't look away until his hand slides under her jeans . . the buttons coming undone just as easily as the ones on her shirt . . his hand moving farther below the waistband of her underwear . . moving like tiny spiders under her clothes until she reaches down and pulls his hand away . . puts it back on her sides where it stays while they keep kissing . . the sound of their lips coming together and coming apart and I wish someone would turn the tv on . . wish someone would start talking to cover up the noise.

I feel him lean into me . . his shoulder leaning into mine . . feel his breath on my neck and feel my bones shake . . thinking he is going to kiss me that way . . that his hand is going to undress me that way and leave me naked for them to watch the way I've been watching. But he whispers to me instead . . –*Maybe we should go in the kitchen or outside or something*– . . and his voice is normal . . he is not growling or dangerous . . and I let his hand touch my hand . . let his arms pull me off the sofa and let him lead me away from this room that smells like the way Avery and Jenna are touching each other.

I feel like a ghost walking out of that room . . so light the way he pulls me along like there is nothing except air inside me . . no bones . . no anything . . and Benji is able to pull me from the room like a boy pulling a balloon . . pulling me up the two tiny steps that lead out of the living room and into the hall by the front door where our shoes are bunched up in a pile . . thrown off our feet to keep the carpet from getting muddy . . pulling me past the pictures that Avery's mother hung on the wall . . family snapshots . . sitting around a birthday cake . . two candles and Avery with chocolate on his baby face . . his mother in an outdated hairstyle and she looks like she is dressed for somebody's wedding that is not her own because those pictures are farther down the hall.

Quickly past every picture like moving quickly through time.

Slowly I can start to feel my toes on the carpet . . sinking in with each step. I can feel the touch of his palm holding all of my fingers together . . leading me into the kitchen where the trees grow so tall and close together in the back-yard that we need to turn the light on to see even though the sun is burning brightly on the pavement out in front of the house.

Benji lets go of my hand and walks over to the refrigera-tor. I am left standing in the middle of the kitchen with the table behind me and the counter in front of me and nowhere to rest my hands . . standing in the center of the room like a museum exhibit with my fingers resting on my lips and the fluorescent light twinkling above me and all that is missing is a glass case and a sign that reads *Lacie*. Nobody is visiting except him and he is busy looking in the refrigerator for something to drink . . and there is a strange feeling inside me . . a feeling like I want him to look at me . . to see me with my hand pressed against my face . . smelling like his hand where he held me . . wanting him to look but not to touch . . like in a museum.

–You want anything to drink?– he asks with his face buried in the shelves. *–Soda okay?–* . . and still I don't say anything because of the strange feeling inside me that makes me forget that he is talking to me . . then his face . .

turning around to look at me and I feel everything dissolve inside me again like I'm made of air . . not heavy like a statue . . like his eyes unfroze me . . turned me from stone into air and I can move again only because he saw me.

–Um . . okay– and he digs again in the refrigerator . . taking out two cans of soda and opening them to the sound of bubbles rushing over the tin tops. He hands me one and I put my lips over it to keep it from spilling . . using my tongue to catch the drops that are about to fall on the floor and I see the way he is watching me . . the same way Avery was watching Jenna in the car . . the same way I was watching them. He looks away when I catch him looking at me like that . . goes over to the table and the chair makes a horrible screeching sound when he pulls it away to sit down.

–You would think they would go to his room to do that.– He cranes his neck in the direction of the living room. –I hate when he does that in front me . . like he's showing off or something.–

I take a sip from the can . . holding it with both hands and the little bubbles tickling my lip . . I stay standing in the middle of the room . . don't go over to him because maybe what he is saying is a trick . . maybe it is just one of those things boys say to make them sound sensitive . .

maybe what he really means is that he wishes it was him and not Avery . . me and not Jenna.

–Doesn't it bother you?– This time he turns to look at me instead of speaking into his hands the way he was speaking . . asking me . . Lacie . . in the center of the kitchen holding a soda with both of my hands and sipping it like a little child sips things so that they don't spill and make a mess. Doesn't it bother me? Jenna beneath him? The way Avery moves his hands over her like petting an animal? Doesn't it bother me?

I think it does but those words don't come out of me. Stuck somewhere inside me because I'm afraid to say them . . afraid of what he will think if I say them . . afraid he will think some of the things I've heard other kids say behind my back . . things like *prude* and *loser*. But I'm also afraid to say it doesn't bother me too because maybe then he'll think he can do those things to me . . that I'm a slut . . and I don't know which I want him to think . . don't know which it is better to be.

–I don't know.– I shrug my shoulders and look at the rim of the soda can with the carbonation bouncing around inside it.

–He's just always showing off about it . . how many girls he gets and how far he gets with them and that kind of stuff– Benji says . . looking out the window into the backyard where a squirrel is climbing one of the trees that stands right outside the house . . staring at it but his eyes are somewhere else and I realize that he hasn't really been talking to me . . more like talking to himself . . to his shaggy-haired reflection in the window where the fluorescent lights hit off it. *–Like he's better than me–* he continues . . shaking his head and then turning to me. *–Rubbing it in my face like there's something wrong with me if I don't . . you know what I mean?–*

His eyes on me . . waiting for me . . wanting for me to say that I know what he means and I want to cry out that I do . . that I know what he means . . know exactly what he means because Jenna is the same . . but holding my mouth pressed against the cold soda can to keep the words in . . to keep from letting out any secrets accidentally.

–Nevermind. It's stupid– he says and looks away from me again.

I am sure he is being honest with me . . that his words are not tricks disguised to fool me. His voice is too clear . .

too honest to be lies. He really feels the way he says and I wonder how he can be so honest with me when he doesn't even know me and I cannot even tell the truth about how I feel to the people who are closest to me. And I think of how wrong I was about what I thought about him . . in the car and in the living room . . thinking he wanted to hurt me when really now I know he didn't. Thinking how I was so sure about it and if I can be wrong about that then maybe I'm wrong about other things. And all of this thinking is happening in short seconds and again the airy feeling like I'm going to faint . . to fall like the leaves from the trees outside when the wind picks up.

He gets up from his chair and leaves it pulled out from the table. *–Forget it–* he says. *–You want to go outside? They have a tv on the porch.–*

–No.–

He drops his head . . his eyes getting sad but that's not it. I want to go outside with him. For the first time ever I want to but it's not that. It's the time . . the way the sun is turning orange and sinking in the clouds.

–I have to go home– I say. *–My little brother . . I have to watch him.–*

–Oh– he says . . looks at me from the corner of his eyes like maybe he doesn't believe me so that I say I'm sorry . . that I really do have a little brother and I really do have to go home. –I can't drive– he says –I'm only a sophomore.– All of a sudden I see him differently than I did before . . I thought . . I mean I assumed he was the same age as Avery . . a senior . . and now that he's only my age except for one more year he isn't as scary to me.

It's my turn to say –oh– and his turn to look shy. Both of us standing in the middle of the room now. Me twisting the ends of my hair around and around . . quickly looking back toward the hall that leads to the living room . . not wanting to walk back in there . . stuttering a little when I say –Okay I'll go ask Avery.–

Tracing my steps back past the photographs pasted on paper behind glass and hung up in frames . . past our shoes where I stop to slip mine on . . to be ready because I'm in a hurry . . to be ready so that they can't ask me to wait five or ten or twenty more minutes. With my shoes on I will only have to peek into the room because I won't want to track any dirt onto the carpet that is white like the furniture . . white like the brick and siding outside . . white like Jenna's skin where her shirt is pulled open over her shoulders and her bra is undone and resting around her waist when I look into the room.

I put my hand up to stop the words from coming from my mouth . . to cover up any sound that might let them know I'm somewhere where I can see them because I can't help but feel like I'm seeing something wrong . . the way Avery's belt is open and his zipper is down . . the way his thing is sticking out and standing up . . Jenna's fingers wrapped around it moving up and down and her face buried under his face and I don't say anything . . don't hear anything except for the soft sounds she makes underneath him . . the hard sounds he makes like a dog panting.

Too terrified to stay standing there . . too terrified to move.

–*I'll walk with you*– I hear Benji say in my ear . . behind me . . hands on my shoulders to back me out of the room and I nod my head over and over as he reaches back and floods the hall with sunlight from the front door opening . . nodding as we step outside into the sound of birds chirping and the last of the summer bees buzzing and the sound of the cars out on the main road off in the distance behind the houses on the other side of the street.

–*Okay*– I say . . saying it too late . . long after we are on the sidewalk already and in front of the house next door . .

letting the sound of my feet settle me . . letting it chase the pictures away that are stuck in my mind the way a camera's flash stays in your eyes. *–Thanks.–* Knowing we have a long way to walk . . knowing that I am going to be late but not caring because I'm just glad to be out of there.

We walk together through the tiny neighborhoods . . the housing developments that are placed so carefully with pretty winding streets and houses just far enough apart so you don't have to know your neighbors. They all have names like *Ramblewood* and *Shady Lanes* and *Fox Run* . . names that make them their own little towns in this bigger little town . . names that make them sound like forests in old stories . . names to make the people who live there forget that this is just the same as every other place.

We cut through the lawns between the houses . . shortcuts around the curving of the streets that give the illusion of distance when you are driving.

We cut across the golf course that sits between two of the developments and connects Avery's to the one where my house is . . cutting through the tot-lots and playgrounds where I see kids Malky's age already riding bikes through the dirty sand. I try to walk faster without running. Walking beside all the houses that are like the miniature houses in my bedroom . . the porcelain houses my father used to bring me whenever he traveled for work . . two from St. Louis . . one from New Orleans . . one from Harrisburg . . five from Chicago and even more from New York . . from all over the place but none from the last two years. So many houses on the highest shelf in my room where I put them away so I wouldn't have to see them . . put them in wherever they fit the same way the houses on these streets seem to be . . stuck in wherever there was enough space . . just enough to be able to look into your neighbor's windows and make sure they are as normal as they are supposed to be.

–*Thanks for walking me all the way*– I say. I haven't said more than two words since we left . . since I saw Jenna lying on the sofa with her eyes closed and her mouth open inside Avery's . . lying there like two dogs and I think of what Avery kept saying . . *Dogboy* . . saying it to Benji and really it was him that was that way . . really it was him that should be called that.

–*Why does he call you that?*– I say . . I have to squint because of the way the sun is . . low in the sky and coming

63

in between me and Benji. I have to squint to see that he is confused . . that he doesn't know what I mean because I was only thinking things again instead of saying them. *–Dogboy? Why does he call you that?–*

Benji pushes his hands into his pockets . . a breeze blows up to us and pulls our hair in front of our eyes. *–I don't know–* he says. *–Because of an old movie or something. The dog was named Benji but I'm named after my grandfather. So I don't know.–* He says Avery started calling him that when he was ten as a joke but now it's sort of like a nickname.

I tell him I don't know that movie so that I'm going to call him *Benji* and he laughs. *–You're not at all like your friend Jenna–* . . and I feel my heart jump inside my rib cage . . feel that panic feeling inside where everything is all tight all of the sudden because I've let myself be calm and I know that is a mistake maybe.

–I'm not?– I need to know what he thinks before I say anything else . . need to know what he means . . need to know if I did something wrong.

–No you're not. No offense but she kind of sucks– he says. I think about the way she laughs when Avery makes a

64

joke . . about the way she tosses her hair back whenever he looks at her . . the way she talks and acts around him and I know what he means. But I tell him she is only like that sometimes . . that she's different when he's not around.

–*That's what I mean!*– Benji says. –*She's different when he's not around . . that's exactly what I mean! Everyone around here is different when someone else isn't around.*–

His eyes get the same way they did in the kitchen . . staring so far away that I can't see where . . staring and it's like he's out there where he's looking even though he is standing right next to me . . walking next to me . . his steps angry . . his hands clenched inside his pockets into fists. I don't know why but I reach over . . I find my way into his pocket and take his hand out the way he took mine to lead me away from that house . . and I don't even feel like me . . I feel strange . . but somehow I feel like I'm myself for the first time . . like I'm not pretending for the first time and this is me that wants to hold his hand.

It is his turn to jump . . when my fingers touch his and his body flinches.

–*Sorry*– he says. –*I don't know. I just hate this town . . I can't wait until I'm old enough to leave and go somewhere*

where people don't judge you right away. Like New York maybe.— And I don't tell him that I'm scared of crowded places . . that there are *too* many people there to stare at you . . to judge you.

I let go of his hand then. I only meant to hold it once . . not forever. I only meant to let him know that I understood him and I think he understands when I let his hand go because he doesn't look surprised or hurt by it . . just puts his hand back in his pocket like it was the most natural thing in the world for us to have held hands like that.

I want to tell him that I know what he means . . that I don't feel like I belong either . . but I can't. I can't let go of my secrets so easily . . not like he can . . not yet . . and I have to keep telling myself that I don't even know him because I feel like I do . . because I know what he means about the way people look at you . . like they look at me since my father killed himself . . like I'm going to break into pieces if they talk too loudly to me. The way they don't want to talk about things that are not comfortable.

I know what he means when he tells me how they look at him . . like he's dirty . . like he's poor and that means he's worthless. The way they look at him because he lives over in *Tricia Meadows* where the houses are all one floor . . a trailer park where the cars in the driveways are not as new and the stuff inside their houses is not as new either. It's the same as they look at me only with me it's not on the outside . . it's not the things I have . . it's inside where I'm broken. But still I know . . I know how alone he feels . . I know but I don't say so with words but I say so with my eyes and he says the same back with his.

*   *   *

I can see my brother in front of our house when we walk onto my street. He is sitting on the front steps . . waiting for me . . not too long though. I'm not so late yet that he is worried.

I'm glad to see him there . . glad because then I won't have to invite Benji inside . . I won't have to lie to him . . won't have to tell him that I don't really want him to. He might not understand . . but I don't have to because Malky is sitting there and I can tell Benji that is why he can't come in if he asks. He never does though . . and I thank him

67

again for walking me home and he asks if I see him in school tomorrow will I talk to him?

I nod.

I will too . . I will talk to him tomorrow and the next day and the next . . just not right now . . not anymore today. I need to be by myself because I feel so much of everything . . I feel so exhausted from the entire day that I have to hurry inside before I start crying from being so exhausted. –Bye– and I wave before I turn around and run up to the door where Malky is asking me why I'm late . . pulling on my sleeve while I try to unlock the door . . asking and asking and I'm not saying anything . . trying to get the door open before I break into tears and I can feel Benji's eyes on me . . can feel him there on the sidewalk watching me.

–Lacie answer me!– Malky whines and I shake his hand off my sleeve . . tell him it's nothing . . tell him I was at Jenna's. –Who's that?– he asks . . his small finger pointing at Benji who starts to back away and I say he's a friend . . he's no one . . to nevermind. And then the door opens and the scent of everything in our house rushes into me like a wave on the beach . . the sweet sour scent of my pillow that is everywhere in our house and I push Malky in and tell

68

him that I will make him something to eat. Then I look
back to see Benji looking at me.

He waves again and I smile . . wave once before the
tears start coming out of my eyes . . before I hurry up inside
and lock the door behind me.

It's almost time for my mother to come home for dinner . . an early night for her the one day a week that we eat together. I should go downstairs and make sure the table is set. I should make sure the dirty dishes are out of the sink and that Malky has cleaned up his toys from the living room . . that his homework is done and checked. I should . . but I can't tear myself away from the miniature houses that I have taken down from my top shelf and spread out all over the floor in my bedroom.

I have arranged them like the houses on my street . . trying to match the order of them so there is a blue house where a blue house should be and a red one where a red one should be. Making it perfect. The way the carpet acts like the lawns and the streets and even the trees. The way there are little people in the windows when I peek through

70

them . . and the people are the same as the people who live in the real houses . . just as fake and painted on . . and all of them probably downstairs right now setting the table and making sure the children have done their homework . . and if I look in the porcelain house that I have set up as mine will I find a girl sitting in her bedroom with the door locked? . . with porcelain houses set up on her floor the way I have done and thinking about how strange the world is? . . thinking how easy it is to put it back together on your floor? . . how simple it must be not to have any feelings?

My brother has knocked on my door two times to tell me Jenna is on the phone. I heard it ringing. I knew it was her each time but I didn't want to talk to her. I don't answer him . . I don't know what to say and so I hear him tell her *—she'll have to call you back she's sleeping.—* Because that's what we say when anyone calls for my mother and she doesn't want to talk to them.

Jenna's calling to say she's sorry for not driving me home on time the way she promised. She's calling to find out what I thought of Avery and to tell me everything they did in that room until she had to be home. She's calling to find out what I did with Benji . . what we did when we were alone and if I kissed him or if I let him touch me . . and I don't feel like talking about that most of all. I don't feel like

71

telling her we didn't do anything and then listen to that sound in her voice when she is disappointed in me. I don't feel like explaining to her that we talked and how that was better probably than what she did . . how he said things with his eyes that I've never heard before.

No. I don't feel like telling her about it. I don't want to have to tell her what we said because she'll just think I'm *being gay*. She'll just think that we only talked because I was too scared to let him do anything to me the way Avery does things to her. And I'm worried I might believe her . . that maybe I am just afraid and maybe I am just trying to cover up for that.

I don't know what to think . . because everything he said makes sense to me but everything Jenna says makes me want to think the way she does . . makes me want to fit in . . makes me want to be like her even though I know I'm not . . even though I'm more like he is but being that way doesn't stop people from talking about you . . being that way doesn't make life easy and I'm tired of everything being so hard.

But in here everything is safe and I am safe from having to be anything. Lying here on my bedroom floor I am safe with the little houses spread all around me. Nothing is going to happen in here. No one is going to say anything about me in here.

I lay my head back on the carpet and see the moon up through my bedroom window . . the sky still blue a little but the moon is there and the sun is still there but on the other side of the house. The moon is there watching me and no one else . . safe in here and I feel for the bottom of my shirt . . feel my hand slipping in under it the way I imagine someone else's would . . pulling my shirt up all the way so that I can feel the breeze from the window on my skin. Moving my hand the way Avery's hand moved . . the way he touched her breast only I leave mine there longer . . pretending the eyes of everyone in those porcelain houses are staring out at me now but still I'm safe here and they can't hurt me.

I don't have to be scared in here . . I don't have to push my hand away the way Jenna had to push his. I don't have to be afraid of the way everything feels on fire inside me where my skin is folded together . . no one is watching except the tiny people in tiny toy houses . . except the moon that is a strange color blue . . Benji's eyes are a strange color blue . . thinking of him watching me lying on my floor . . thinking of him and I pinch down harder but it's okay because I'm safe in here . . secrets are safe in here.

Letting my jeans fall open . . letting them fall around my knees and I hear one or two or maybe more of the houses being pushed out of the way. Feeling around inside me . . feels warm and safe like my room and maybe Benji is right and maybe all those people are wrong and there is nothing wrong with me and only things wrong with them.

Like this on my floor . . lying open like this . . inside myself . . there is nothing wrong. Soon though my mother will be home . . and I will have to pretend today like I pretend any other day.

We will all pretend we are like any of the other families on the street . . we will pretend our house is like those miniature houses that I kick every time I move. We will pretend we are perfect . . eating dinner as a family . . pretending my father didn't go crazy and make himself dead in the bathtub . . pretend that my mother doesn't work all the time so that she can avoid being here where he did it . . so she can avoid Malky who reminds her too much of him . . pretend that Malky is normal without her around . . that he doesn't need her around . . pretend that he is like the other kids his age and forget that he wets the bed or that he never talks about any friends . . pretend that I am normal . . that I'm not scared every time I open my eyes and see the world staring at me . . pretend all those things while we eat and smile and say nice things.

I don't want to pretend anymore. I don't want to feel like one of those people in the tiny toy houses. I want to feel real like the way I feel lying here on the floor . . naked with my skin on fire and the breeze coming in off the moon. I want to feel the way I felt when Benji held my hand. I want to feel that way all the time . . forever.

I hear her car pull up.

I take my fingers out of my mouth . . pull my shirt down and bring my underwear up.

I hear the front door open and close and my brother running up to her. *–Mommy's home!–* and I can feel her backing away from his hug . . can see her remembering my dad in the way Malky smiles and it makes me shiver.

I button up my jeans and quickly straighten my clothes so that it doesn't look like I've been lying on the floor . . see

my messy hair in the mirror and push the loose black curls
back into place.

–*Lacie?*– my mother calls and I unlock my bedroom
door and close it again behind me . . call down that I'll be
there in a second and then rush into the bathroom to wash
my hands.

day 29

Today is the day he kissed me.

Today is a day that will stay with me forever . . the twi-light breaking through the clouds . . gray clouds like rain . . so low they are all around us . . in our hands . . our hands holding the clouds and holding each other.

Today is the day he walks with me from the school like we planned . . my mother home early on her day off and we planned it all week like this. Together . . alone. Walking away from the school buildings and past the fields where the soccer teams and football teams and field hockey teams are all running little races that go nowhere . . getting far-ther away from them so they don't look any bigger than the miniature people in my miniature town . . so many of them running in the distance like ants crawling over ice-cream cones in the sand . . so many of them but it is only the two of us in the world it seems.

He talks about big cities he's never been to . . talks about them like their buildings are dreams that can be lived in . . telling me the words he's read about them . . perfect pretty words that are so unlike the way the houses are placed on my street. His eyes light up when he talks about those places . . about the amazing things he imagines happening on every corner . . the different kinds of people and the different ways of talking . . about how he could feel at home in those places . . his eyes growing wider than there is space for . . growing brighter than all the stars that are drawn in the night.

—It's like the places you draw in your pictures— he tells me and I blush . . tell him it is nothing like that . . like my pictures of the broken walls in old castles . . the lonely girl in her torn dress . . her hand begging for change though she used to be a princess. Benji says it is. *—It's just like that . . it's like any place . . just depends on how you imagine it.—*

Then he moves next to me . . and it is so easy to let him take my other hand . . to hold both of them and let him face me . . let him stare at me . . liking the way he is look-

80

ing at me like he wants to see under my skin and through my bones and see that part of me that will become a ghost someday.

He lets go of my hands . . and I want him to . . knowing he wants to . . moving his hands up to touch my face . . letting mine fall in front of me . . letting my head bow because I feel weak. I want him to lift my chin to look at him . . to look at the dried cornfields behind him that stretch out as far as the sky . . the farmhouse somewhere in the middle of all that . . surrounded by three trees that have changed color . . the last thing I see before I close my eyes . . our mouths open when our lips touch.

Today is the day he kissed me.

And when he kisses me I feel the world around me . . feel everything the way I've never felt before . . the wind on my arms and through every wavy strand of hair blowing behind me. I feel perfectly still the way the stars must feel when the sun passes by. Then when he leans toward me . . when he presses his body against mine and his hands slide so softly from my face and down my shoulders around my arms and when he pulls me closer with his hands resting on the small of my back . . I feel something else then.

I feel everything that is him crawl inside me . . inside my mouth . . first I feel sick in my stomach like there was too much inside me . . his thoughts and his dreams inside me . . tangled up with mine. I put my arms around him to hold on . . to keep from spinning and falling and getting lost in all of the feelings that are swaying inside me the way the fields of grain sway in the summertime. And when he pulls away I feel him still there . . inside me . . like he is there with all I touch and all I see and there is not even air that separates the ghosts inside us because they have grown to look alike and be alike and they lie on top of each other and inside each other and when I open my eyes I think I know how it is to be in love.

–I . . I . . – he stutters but I shake my head.

Please don't speak. Please don't say anything.

Later in my room I will draw him like that . . standing there with the brown fields behind him . . the twilight straining behind the clouds and the clouds hanging low on the ground . . the wind blowing his hair in his face but his eyes so strong that they shine . . memorizing every tint of every color . . memorizing every line . . memorizing it for-ever.

Before I run I smile at him . . smile a way I have never smiled . . not hiding anything . . not keeping anything for only myself and smiling at him the way women smile . . before I run.

Laughing with arms at my sides like a scarecrow . . running through the tall stalks of dead corn . . my hands banging against every one on either side only I don't feel a thing . . only feel the things inside . . like tiny stars exploding over and over . . a way I've never felt . . or haven't felt in so long . . running.

Running to chase the sun out of the sky.
Running to catch up with it but it moves too far.
Running because that is how I feel today.

Today. The day he kissed me. Today. The day I met me. *Lacie Joanna Johnson.*

day 41

The swing squeaks on its chains . . back and forth . . squeaking in the empty playground. The echo carries across the lawn . . across the baseball field and over into the woods. I have my toes in the sand . . pushing myself on the swing . . more like rocking . . back and forth watching the cars go by on the road in front of my old elementary school . . listening to the creaking of rusted chains between my fingers.

The school building is empty . . the kids are gone . . the teachers gone too. Only the janitor is around . . pushing his broom through the halls that smell like paste . . pushing a mop in the bathrooms that smell like little kids. I like watching the way he walks with his back bent over . . bending forward each time the swing squeaks . . the classrooms dark with twilight . . shadows over the alphabet charts . . shadows sitting at the desks.

The classrooms are all decorated with pumpkins carved into faces . . bats made from construction paper . . ghosts made from sheets with black marks drawn on for the eyes. It all seems so happy in the decorations. The haunting characters seem so safe and harmless. The scary things not scary when done on purpose. Nothing like the real ghosts that crawl into windows at night . . not like real demons that crawl into souls and make them sad.

The swing goes higher each time I bend my knees . . higher and higher . . my feet in front of me to push the clouds out of the way . . to push memories farther away . . not on top of me like they are now.

I don't want to think about things that make it so I can't be happy.

I want to think about the way the end of the daylight sits on the top of fallen leaves . . raked into piles red and brown and gold.

I want to think about Benji walking with his hands in his

jacket . . pulling the collar closed at his neck where the zipper is broke . . blowing on his hands when the wind picks up too cold . . coming to meet me.

I don't want to think about bad things anymore.
I don't want to think about ghosts anymore.

But the ghosts have a way of always coming back . . of haunting you even when you are wide awake . . even when you are concentrating so hard to not let them find their way into you.

They always find you. They always know where you are . . waiting. They know when you are in your room at night with the blanket thrown around your feet . . with your nightgown open for them to come to you . . to cover your skin and drench it white with fear . . wrapping it so deep to lick your bones and make you scream so loud that your mother rushes in to find you afraid and naked and unable to explain what was so near to you only seconds ago.

Sometimes they find you in memories. They eat away at what you used to know and find out where they can live in your past. And they cast themselves in the events you want to remember . . not just the ones you want to forget.

That's why I don't want to remember anything . . I want to wake up tomorrow and be someone who I never was before . . be a new Lacie that never had bad things happen and maybe then I can be happy with the good things that happen to me. Then I wouldn't be the person sitting on a child's swing crying as the sun goes down behind the trees . . crying without making any sounds . . crying when I should be jumping up and down at the sight of the boy I like walking around the curve in the street several hundred yards away.

I don't want to be her anymore.

I don't want to be the girl whose father killed himself two years ago today.

The swing goes higher and higher and maybe if I just let go of the chains . . let myself fly off the edge of the world . . if I float up to the stars and never come back down then all the pain would go away.

My fingers unwrap themselves one by one.

My hands let go of the chains.

The clouds come down to touch me . . the trees wave their branches like the skinny bones of a skeleton . . the ground has nothing to weigh me down . . no gravity . . and it is so easy not to scream . . it is so easy to enter the sky . . it is so easy to fly.

But they are there. The ghosts are there with me.

They will never let me go so easily . . clawing at my throat . . claws across my chest to pull me back . . calling me back with memories of places and people and things that happened slightly different than they look in photographs . . things that happened before but something about what is happening now is the same . . same enough to make me remember . . being a child . . jumping off swings and landing with my chin in the dirt . . losing my first tooth there with my fingers covered in dried blood . . blood on my sleeve . . under my fingernails . . and then he was there to pick to me up . . to carry me home and help me wash my face . . to help me place the tooth under my pillow at night and to help me share a dollar in the morning when I woke up.

Memories as I'm falling. The playground is littered with memories beneath me . . sprouting up like trees so that they make it impossible to see the present . . populating the swing set with someone who used to be me . . populating the school with voices of kids that have stopped being kids . . populating the entire scenery with ghosts of what used to be.

They make me remember these things . . the ghosts all around me. It hurts to remember . . like poison . . knowing that he will always be in them and that he will never be here.

He is not here now to pick me up.

He is nowhere. He is the ghost that grabs my hands and tugs me back to earth . . pulling me down so that my feet slip on the cold ground . . so that my head hits against the hard sand and the air rushes out of me in one gulp and I can almost see the ghost hands hovering above my mouth waiting for my breath to leave me . . pale hands like trails of smoke trying to snatch my soul when I get the wind knocked out of me.

I close my eyes . . not sure if I want to live or if I want to die.

*　　*　　*

Beneath my head his arms feel like the sand . . taking the shape of me . . bending in all the right places to help me up . . to lift my head . . pull my knees to my chest and open my eyes to let the twilight in.

The clouds move by so fast . . shifting and growing . . spreading out thinner and thinner to cover the last of the blue in the sky . . moving so fast like a movie sped up on the television . . frame by frame . . like stuttering almost and I wonder if I am really awake.

–Lacie? You okay?–

But I'm looking up at the sky . . the clouds moving across it like spilled milk moving across a tiled floor. I'm not looking at Benji kneeling beside me . . helping me to sit up without falling down . . holding my hands in his and the only thing I notice is how warm his hands are from blowing on them . . how cold mine are from the autumn wind.

–For a second . .– whispering the words not so much to him but to the clouds . . not so much saying them but thinking them with my mouth . . never finishing them out loud . . the part about flying . . for a second it felt like that.

He uses the sleeve of his flannel shirt to wipe the corners of my mouth where I must have bitten through my lip a little when I hit the ground. I pull away the black strands of

hair that are caught in my mouth and push them aside . .
turn my eyes to him . . my mouth open slightly . . not to
speak . . only to breathe . . the squeaking of the swing
behind me.

Benji's face looks so serious . . the way he moistens his
sleeve to wipe at the scrapes on my hands . . thin red
scratches where the chain slid over my skin. His eyes nar-
row . . concentrating . . the way my eyes get when I'm taking care of Malky . . the way anyone's eyes get when they
care for someone.

I don't feel a thing. Not the scratches. Not my lip that is
still bleeding. Not the fear that I felt just a moment ago
when the ghosts were hovering over me.

Nothing.

I'm numb all the way through like the way I feel when
I'm running . . when I run so fast that my sneakers never
touch down on the pavement.

I want to run now . . to never stop . . to run always.

Then I start to feel again . . the world coming to touch

94

me piece by piece like being able to feel single raindrops in a storm . . feeling the way my hands sting . . feeling the cut on my lip . . feeling all of that separate from the feel of his hand against my cheek.

He is staring at me . . trying to stare into some hidden place inside me where I hide things from him . . from everybody.

His eyes are so calm . . bluer than any colors on the television . . nothing stirring in them and they are perfectly still . . perfectly beautiful like snapshots of hurricanes taken from satellites so far away that you can forgive them any damage they may cause later.

I wonder what he must see in mine . . so muddy brown that it is impossible to tell where the black begins and the brown ends without the right light . . nothing calm . . seeing the static inside me . . seeing the need to keep running and running because if I never make any more memories then I can be sure that there will never be any bad ones.

I don't know how many words he has said before I hear him . . before I let them come in . . before I let myself understand them.

–What were you doing?– he asks and I realize he is talking about the swing . . about me jumping off and making no attempt to land.

I was communicating with ghosts.
I was losing my first tooth for the second time.
I was trying not to go back in time two years.
I was trying to fly up to the clouds where there is a fallen castle waiting for me to return because it thinks I'm its princess.

I never dare tell him the answers. I never dare share that many secrets. He would never love me if he knew.

–Nothing . .– I say. *–Just . . falling–*

I watch the way his hair comes untucked behind his ear when he shakes his head . . covers his eyes and I feel dizzy without their calm. But then he laughs . . just once . . not the way people laugh in the movies . . not the way Jenna laughs when someone wears the wrong thing . . not like he is acting. *–You should be more careful when you fall–* he says and then laughs again . . something kind about it . . something calm.

I think then that he is going to kiss me again . . sense

him leaning into me so slowly that it is not something I can see. I have to keep myself from pulling away . . have to keep myself from doing something more that will make him think I'm crazy . . something more than falling from the swing.

Either he can feel my reluctance or else he never was . . because he doesn't . . he never even tries.

He hasn't kissed me since the first time and I'm not sure what that means . . maybe it means that he already doesn't like me anymore . . maybe it means he likes me enough to know how scared I am of everything.

Jenna told me it means something else. She told me I must kiss like a frog or else he would have tried again . . told me boys always try again . . over and over . . try anything they can to get farther.

–*It's not true*– I said and she said yes it was . . again she said I kiss like a frog and made her mouth open wide with her tongue wagging out . . made noises the way little kids make noises when they talk about kissing and that made Kara laugh and made Mandy call me –*Frog girl*– . . Frog girl and Dogboy and they had a lot of fun with that . . teasing me like 5th graders tease and I wanted to remind Jenna . . wanted to say about how she was the one who taught me . . about that day last year when she showed me how to kiss . . but I didn't say anything. I knew she would only make it worse if I did.

–*Maybe it's him though!*– she said . . her eyes glowing like a wolf that comes upon an animal that's already trapped . . seeing a new way to make Kara and Mandy laugh . . –*Maybe he's gay . . Maybe he doesn't even like girls*– then laughing when my face went all red . . saying she could ask Avery for me . . that she could find out for me.

–NO DON'T!– I said.

–*Why not? Don't you want to know? I mean . . either way you need to know.*– I kept shaking my head. –*You don't want a gay boyfriend! And you don't want to be the WORST kisser in the world either.*–

She waved over to Avery . . waved him to come over to where we were sitting and I begged her . . with each step closer I begged her . . crossed my fingers so tight.

–*Avery*– she said . . her voice faking that it was serious . . –*Lacie wants to ask you something.*–

–Yeah?– he said looking at her . . never looking at me . . at the way I was bent over . . the sickness in my stomach.

–Go ahead Lacie!– Jenna said. I kept my face down . . kept shaking my head . . begging inside my head for her to stop and putting my fingers up to my mouth . . *–Oh never-mind–* she said.

She apologized later . . said it was only for fun . . that I shouldn't take things so seriously. And I know that . . I know she was only playing around . . teasing the way I see them always tease each other about boys.

But what if she's right?

What if I am the worst . . what if he doesn't like me? What if I am just the ugly girl that no one will ever like . . if everything he makes me feel is not real the way I want it to be . . if it is only me and not him that feels it?

But he's here . . touching my face . . my blood on his clothes. Maybe he did like it when we kissed . . maybe he is waiting to do more the next time though . . maybe you only kiss once before you let them touch you in other places . . I don't know . . I don't know how boys like to do things. I only know how I do things . . slow.

–Do you ever want to kiss me again?– and my words are taken away by a motorcycle traveling too fast down the lane . . taken away by the wind blowing over the playground and my words get lost somewhere in the fallen leaves . . lost somewhere in the echo off the empty building.

I shouldn't have said anything . . he is too quiet and I know I shouldn't have. I want to run . . run until my shoes wear out and I end up on the other side of the world where no one speaks the way I do. It was stupid to say . . I sound totally crazy . . too crazy for him to ever love.

He takes his hand away from my face and I feel my heart break.

But then . . slowly . . his arm . . pulling away . . setting it behind him . . leaning slowly into me . . his eyes closed . . his eyelashes like a girl's the way they are pretty . . I close my eyes . . let his lips touch mine . . let his tongue touch mine . . and kiss him the way that feels right and forget about anything that Jenna ever said . . anything she ever showed me . . and when we kiss I feel normal.

There is nothing wrong in the world for just one second and everything is perfect.

He stands up quickly . . holds his hand out to help me up. *–Come on . . let's go–* . . and we walk together off the playground. We still have two hours before it is dark . . two hours until I have to be home.

I let him lead . . let him pull on my hand to wherever he wants to go . . everything stills . . feels too empty around me . . like every step is another step into a dream.

The houses get farther behind us . . their backyard fences become harder to see through the trees growing as close as they want to . . that are not planted exactly three feet apart here in the woods . . here on the trail that leads down to the creek that runs behind my development . . our shoes following the dirt path leading into it . . into the shadows where the sun is lost above us . . where the wind isn't as strong but where the cold has set in and found places to live in the dark corners under the leaves.

I worry that we will go too far . . wonder if we should stop or turn around or anything because if it gets too dark we won't be able to find our way out. Benji tells me not to worry . . that he comes here all the time and that there is something he wants to show me . . not too far . .

–What if it gets dark? Won't we get lost?–

Benji laughs . . I don't like it that he laughs . . that he is laughing at me . . at what I said . . I don't know what is funny about being scared . . about being lost and never being found again.

I pull my hand away.
I fold my arms in front of me and refuse to take another step.

–Lacie!– and he tries to pull me forward but I only turn my head . . *–We can't get lost . . walk in any direction and you're going to run into a house or a shopping center or a mall or one of the other million things they build every-where–* he says.

–Oh– biting my lip . . holding my hand over my mouth . . wishing I had only thought about it. I guess if I thought about it I would have known that we could never get lost here . . that all around us is the town . . are the stores that sell the same things only with different names on

the door. This isn't a fairy tale where evil things live in the forest . . this isn't even a forest and if you listen carefully you can hear the cars on the highway that cuts through the middle of all the trees not too far ahead of us . . you can hear the electricity racing through the power lines above the trees.

—*It still doesn't mean I want to go*— I whisper . . because I'm not really supposed to . . at least I wasn't before when I was younger. Maybe it's okay now. I'm old enough now to make up my own rules . . but not without letting anyone know . . not alone.

—*Come on*— Benji says walking ahead of me . . waving me to follow.

I wonder what he wants to show me . . I wonder if this is how he plans to see me naked . . if we are alone and no one is around . . if that is how it works. That's how all the horror stories start . . going where you don't want to . . trusting someone. But I guess that is what trust is all about . . giving in . . not being so safe all the time.

He stops when he notices I'm not following him . . his expression asking me so many questions. There are so many trees . . so many shadows . . but I can see his eyes

104

through them all . . so warm and I know that I can trust him . . that I need to trust him.

–*I didn't mean to laugh*– he says to me when I start walking again . . says he wasn't teasing me. I tell him to never-mind . . I was just being stupid.

Benji points out whenever a puddle is ahead of us so that I can step around it. I've missed too many though and already I can feel the water seep into my socks. In the sunlight that dips in between the pine needles I can see that my sneakers are already ruined . . that the white is stained with too much mud to get clean again.

I don't even see it until he points it out . . I'm too busy looking up at the way the dead branches crisscross over the sky . . twisting around one another like snake sticks . . like knives stabbing at the sun . . so many branches like telephone poles along the streets. I almost trip when he stops . . when I run into him . . my head is bent up to watch the clouds bring winter across the sky.

–*Isn't it great?*– he asks after he has caught me . . after I have my balance . . but I don't know what he sees. I have to follow the direction of his eyes . . follow their glance through the thornbushes and the tree trunks . . through the evergreens until I see a few cinder blocks piled on top of one another about 3ft. high.

I let my eyes drift back farther . . see the other bricks on either side . . see past the shrubs and see that there are four walls only half-built . . the space for windowsills . . for a door . . the pile of brick is part of a house that has never been finished . . or maybe was finished but has been stripped down to its skeleton like the trees with their sticks and branches and their leaves in piles all over the ground.

Benji has walked off in front of me and I try to match where his feet went . . stepping between thornbushes that stick to my jacket and stick to my skin and will tear both if I'm not careful. He knows every step to take . . says he's taken them a million times since he was little.

When I catch up to him he is standing in the doorway that has no door . . looking into the house that has no roof . . no walls other than the four crumbling walls on the outside . . no floor except the sunken ground with over-grown weeds and a rusty lawn chair.

–This is the place where I always go . . when I want to be alone . . you know– he says and I pretend that it means exactly what he says . . pretend that isn't as special as it

really is . . pretend that my heart doesn't warm . . that my face is only blushing from the cold. I keep it inside and pretend . . but inside I know this is his way of telling me a secret.

He steps down into the house . . reaching back to help me because years and years of rain have caused the floor to sink below.

I don't move from where he puts me and he gets worried that he shouldn't have taken me here . . that I don't understand what he means and he starts to apologize . . says —*I guess it's not that special . . I just thought maybe . .*— and I put my hand up to my mouth and shake my head.

—*It's like a castle*— I say and then I smile . . it is like a castle in my dreams . . a castle forgotten by everything . . no one in the world exists except me and him . . except us alone . . and here we can pretend that he is a prince . . that I am not Lacie . . that I'm the princess just like the way I draw myself.

I want to stay forever in here. I want the way out of these woods to be forgotten . . to be lost forever and time to stand still for us . . where no one can see us . . can see the way we are in love . . the way his hands fit on my body or the way mine fit on his. We could be each other's own secrets then . . we could be safe from ghosts and things that try to harm us . . we could be safe from the past too . . safe from time altogether.

But I know it can't be that way . . the sun is setting too fast for it to be that way . . the shadows getting longer across our faces . . my hands getting harder to find without feeling for them . . my feet getting colder from the water that has soaked through . . and after a little while we both know it's time to leave . . that in the houses behind us the lights have all turned on . . that the cars have all pulled into driveways and the televisions have come to life.

I need to get home . . my mother is home with Malky . . she is making dinner and I need to be home for them . . I need to be home to try to be a family again. It is important to her that we try to be a family . . especially on this day . . the day that our family fell apart.

–*I have to go home*– I tell Benji . . his arms wrapped around me . . my face buried in his sleeve.

I haven't told him what today is . . I planned on telling him . . wanted to tell him but now it seems wrong to tell him . . doesn't seem as important as it did before . . that what happened two years ago doesn't matter as much as what happens today. Nothing he could say would make me feel any better than he has already made me . . nothing he could do would be more perfect than what he has already done . . so I decide to keep that part to myself for now.

*　　*　　*

I walk so slowly back to my house . . never really wanting to get there. Airplanes flying above me . . everyone on board in such a hurry to get somewhere and way down here I'm trying my best to be impossibly slow.

It's just that when I get home it all will be different . . the afternoon will peel away with each tick of the clock over the fireplace . . the smell of his clothes will fade from my sweatshirt . . the place where he held my arm will go numb and I won't be able to remember exactly where each of his fingers were. Already it is like I haven't seen him for days and he has only just left me to go back to the trailer on the other side of town where he lives.

When I go home all those things from before will still be there to haunt me . . my mother will be waiting for me . . trying to smile . . pretending she doesn't remember the things we can't forget. She will want me to pretend too. She won't want me to talk about those things . . says part of moving on is keeping silent and so I will have to swallow back my words when I get home . . I'll have to close my eyes tight . . cross my fingers . . concentrate on being okay.

I can see the lights on in the kitchen as I get closer. I know it is supposed to make me feel warm . . that it is supposed to seem safe from the darkness outside . . but the long shadows are comfortable . . the late autumn air keeps me from breaking down . . keeps my bones still and I'm afraid I might melt under the electricity if I step inside.

I can see my mother in the kitchen . . still in her robe from this morning . . her hair not even pulled back the way she usually fixes it . . she runs her hand through it and lets it stay where it falls. I doubt she has been out of bed for more than an hour before now. I doubt she has been out of bed for more than two hours the whole day. It's a sick day for her . . an anniversary of being sick that she insists we observe by pretending it never happened . . or at least we don't mention that it ever happened with words but every movement she makes shows that we are never too far away from it. It shows in the creases the sheets have left on her face . . the redness in her eyes . . in the way she pushes the food around in the pan to keep it from burning.

I wish I didn't have to do this . . not today . . this dinner where we sit around and listen to our forks scrape across the plates and to the sound of each other chewing . . saying nothing. We haven't been a family in so long that we don't even remember how to play at it.

We've never really been a family . . not like the families they show in the movies . . not that I can remember. It isn't just since my father died either . . it was before then too . . the way they argued . . the way I would hide by keeping my eyes on my plate and my hands under my legs. It was always the same . . we were always the same . . my father doing what he did only made me realize how many things were wrong with the rest of us too.

Sometimes I think it's almost better since he escaped. There's less to hide from . . less to worry about. We don't have to pretend to be normal so much . . not with each other anyway since usually we are by ourselves. We only have to be a certain way when she's home. That's not too often. But it gets harder to each time . . harder to hide myself from her . . harder to only show her the parts of me that she wants to know. I wish she was never around.

I never thought I would think like that . . that I wouldn't need her here to tell me everything is okay . . to make promises. Now it seems she only reminds me of the things that are wrong with me . . with us . . things I don't want to think about so every day I find myself hoping she will be a little later . . that she will drive a little slower . . to take a little less time off. Maybe that's selfish . . but maybe if she had been around more when I wanted her around it would be different . . maybe then I wouldn't find it so hard to be myself when she is home.

The air rushes out when I open the door. It is like opening the oven . . the warmth making me feel the cold in my hands for the first time . . my fingers have turned pink and inside my sneakers my toes are frozen solid. My ears sting and I have to press my palms to them . . muffling the noise Malky makes taking out the dishes . . the sound of my mother's voice calling out into the hallway . . –*Lacie? Dinner will be ready in just a few minutes. Wash up.*–

Already the way I felt before is disappearing. Already that is gone . . already I want him back again . . it scares me how much I want him right at this moment.

–*Take your shoes off before you go upstairs*– my mother calls out and I want to run away at the sound of her voice. It is only a small feeling . . one that will pass if I let it.

The laces are wet and the knot is too tough so I have to just slip them off . . then I slip off my socks because the water has stained them with mud too. I head up the stairs to my room . . remembering to breathe . . to calm down . . to not look at the bathroom door that is closed as I slip into my bedroom . . slip off my jeans that are wet around the ankles and put something else on.

My mother calls for me . . –*I'm coming*– I say . . quiet enough so that she doesn't hear me.

I look in the mirror . . try to see me behind the black hair and brown eyes . . the few brown freckles on my cheeks . . holding my bottom lip in with my top teeth . . trying to see what he sees when he looks at me . . just for a second before slipping into an ordinary girl again and slipping down to the table where they are waiting for me.

My mom's eyes look cracked . . like a glaze over them has been chipped away in places . . and her eyes are red too the way mine get when I watch too much tv in one day. It makes her smile seem even worse . . sadder I guess.

–Enjoy– she says . . folding her hands over her plate and waiting for us to each pick up our forks and try the meal she has made.

I want to tell her that I'm not hungry.
I want to go to my room and lock the door.

I try not to look at either of them as I eat. My mom is not eating at all . . just sitting there with her hands folded like she is praying . . watching both of us as we eat . . watching us chew and I make sure to chew with my mouth closed because I know how it upsets her if I don't.

From the corner of my eye I can see Malky is smiling . . he is the only one too young to know how awkward it is in the room . . he is the only one who doesn't know what my mother means when she asks –How is it?– . . that she isn't really asking how the food is . . that she is really only trying to fight through the silence.

–It's delicious Mom!– and he smiles wider than he

should hoping that she will be happy with him . . hoping that she will pay him some attention. She only grins at him . . nods and then we return to silence.

It is a few minutes before she tries again . . trying another question. *–What did you do this afternoon?–* she asks. I only shrug my shoulders . . mumble through the food . . *–nothing–* . . and hope she moves on to something else because I haven't told her about Benji yet.

–Did you go over to Jenna's?– resting her chin on her folded hands. I keep my eyes down and nod. She picks up her fork for the first time and smiles. *–Are you lying?–* she says as she places the fork in her mouth.

I can feel the color rushing to my face . . can feel the way my heart screams inside me . . feel my feet tapping on the floor ready to run up the stairs . . knowing I should have run when I felt it . . that I never should have come home today . . every part of me wanting to escape to my room . . safe behind a locked door.

–Jenna called– she says. *–I know you weren't with her.–*

–Oh . . I– stuttering through the knots in my stomach and hating the feeling . . but more than the feeling in my

stomach I hate the way they are both staring at me . . the way my mother raises one eyebrow like a teacher would . . the way she asked just to get me to lie . . the way she is trying to care at all about what I do when she hasn't cared for so long.

–*Where did you go?*– she asks me again . . her voice trying to sound friendly the way I hear it sound when she is talking to a client at the office.

–*I know! I know!*– Malky says when I don't say anything . . his tongue pushing out of his mouth ready to burst at the chance of getting her attention . . of being a tattle-tale . . of being her favorite even for a little bit.

I flash him a quick look . . he better not.

–*She was with her* boyfriend– he teases. I hiss at him . . warning him that he better stop before he says anything else. But he doesn't care about what I say when she's around . . I'm only the substitute mom . . I'm only second-best. –*I bet they were kissing!*– and he starts to laugh and kiss his arm.

–*SHUT UP!*– I snap. I have never been so angry at him before . . I've never wanted to hurt him before the way I want to now . . how I want to pinch his cheek until he starts to cry instead of laugh. He knows that Benji is a secret . . he promised not to tell.

I give him a mean look . . one to let him know that the next time he doesn't want me to tell her something he better not tell me in the first place.

I can't look at her . . her mouth open . . staring at me so deep that I can feel her looking for something hidden behind my skin. I'm sure my mother is going to yell . . that she is going to punish me.

–*Who is this boy?*– my mother asks . . she doesn't yell . . but I can hear that thing in her voice that tells me she hates him . . that she doesn't even have to know him to hate him more than she's ever hated anyone before.

–*He's just a friend*– I whisper . . not daring to look up . . not daring to uncross my fingers pressed under my knee. She wants to know his name and I whisper that too. She complains that she can't hear me . . for me to look at her when I speak and I look up from my plate . . say his name carefully . . finding it hard to make my tongue move the right way like his name is a complicated phrase in a foreign language . . like my mouth is swollen . . but it's my eyes that are swollen . . that are red and itchy . . careful of not saying too much because she won't understand and I hate the way she's staring at me like she wants me to start crying.

She wants to know where he lives . . what his last name is . . if she knows him. But I won't tell her . . won't mention that he lives in those trailers at the end of town because she will say *—you know how I feel about those people—* . . that's what she calls them . . *those people* . . and I want to ask her what makes them any worse than us . . what is better about her never being here to pay for this house that only keeps the ghosts inside us and keeps us from ever being happy.

—He's just a friend!— I don't want to have to hear her say bad things about him . . I don't want her to ask me questions about him every day . . about whether or not he's been in the house when she was gone . . about whether or not I let him touch me. I just want her to pretend she never heard his name and leave me alone about him.

—We'll talk about this more later— she says once I can't keep that first tear in . . when she sees I'm not going to tell her the things she wants to know. But she means it . . that we're going to talk about it some more . . once Malky is in

bed maybe . . that she is going to give me rules to follow . . that she is going to say I can't see him . . that I can't love him anymore.

She turns away from me . . shaking her head to let me know she's disappointed.

–*How was school today?*– she asks Malky . . forcing herself to smile at him . . forcing her voice to be cheerful for him . . ignoring me . . leaving me to sulk . . leaving me to put my fingers in my mouth.

My mother looks at me . . her face smiling at Malky but her eyes on me . . tired and angry.

She reaches over . . toward me.

I flinch.

I close my eyes. Her fingers wrap around my wrist . . her hands so cold . . squeezing . . pulling my arm away from my face . . pulling my fingers out of my mouth and I feel the skin scratch open on my teeth. –*Act your age!*– my mom says . . dropping my hand and letting it fall to the table.

Malky has stopped smiling . . his eyes wide . . afraid of the look on my mom's face . . at the violence in her wrist as it shakes from letting go of my hand . . the little bit of blood on my upper lip.

I'm too startled to move . . to say anything.

Everything in my mother's expression changes . . softens . . her eyes weaken and they aren't angry anymore only tired. She brings her hand to her face . . her wrist still shaking . . trying to form the words . . to apologize but I don't even care.

I hate her!

I don't even try to pretend . . don't try to hold the tears in as I push my chair away from the table.

–Lacie . . I'm sorry . . I– but I'm not listening . . I'm running up the stairs . . choking and sobbing . . slamming the door behind me . . shutting the rest of the world out of my life . . hiding my face in my pillow and promising never to talk to her again.

day 47

Every day can be perfect. Every day can be better than the last day as long as I can see him. As long as we get to walk home together . . as long as he comes inside my house . . inside my bedroom . . lies on my bed and we hold each other and tell our secrets. I don't care what my mother says. I don't care if she doesn't *allow* it because it is the only thing that makes my days perfect.

I can pretend we are the only two people who ever lived . . the window closes out the sounds from outside so that there is only the sound of him breathing.

We share a little more every day.
We tell a little more that we have never told.

He tells me about his mother . . about the way she has a new boyfriend every month. I tell him about the way my mother stays a little farther away every week.

–She picks them up at the bar where she works . . brings them home and sometimes they stay and sometimes they don't.–

I ask him what they're like and he says *–mean–* . . says the ones who stay are meaner . . says that they never really like him. He gets in the way when they are around and that is why he has to hide in that house he found in the woods.

I don't ask him about his dad because I don't want him to ask about mine. I know his is gone . . divorced . . he knows mine is dead and that is all we need to know. So we talk only about mothers . . about the way they seem to wish they weren't mothers at all . . about how sometimes we wish they weren't either.

–I think she hates it here– I tell him. *–I think one day she will just not come back.–*

He wants to know if I talk to her about it and I tell him that I haven't talked to her in six days . . that she doesn't lis-ten . . that talking to her is not like talking to him . . that we never talk about things that are uncomfortable and he says that he and his mom only say uncomfortable things . . they only yell.

–I think she hates me.– I tell him *–I think she thinks I'm crazy . . I think everyone thinks I'm crazy.–* The words hurt to say them out loud . . get caught in my throat on the way out and hurt sitting there. They hurt because I know they are true. I know there is something wrong with me.

Then he touches me . . first on my arm and then on my face . . his hand on my stomach and the hurtful things begin to melt away . . like our words are some kind of spell and as long as we speak them to each other nothing can hurt ever again.

Whispering things to me . . about how there is nothing wrong with me and only wrong with them if they don't see how beautiful I am.

And when we lie on my bed like this it is like everything is perfect in the whole world. There isn't anyone telling me to do things I shouldn't. There isn't anyone else around making me feel like everything I do is wrong somehow. There aren't any nightmares when I close my eyes. There aren't any mothers. There aren't any fathers. There aren't any friends.

There is nothing.

There is only him and there is only me.

There is only happiness but happiness scares me.

Happiness makes me hold on tight to him . . never wanting him to go home in the evening . . never wanting him to leave my side . . never wanting a second without him because when he is not near enough to touch I am terrified I will lose him.

Waiting for it all to break apart again the way my life always breaks apart. Wondering how long he can like me . . how long he will wait for me to let his hand move below my stomach . . wondering if he will even care once he gets to know all of me.

* * *

Sometimes when you're dreaming it takes longer to wake up . . the things in your dream don't want to fade away as fast as your eyes want them to and you're left somewhere in between being awake and still dreaming.

That's where I am . . somewhere in between.

The things in my dream have not disappeared completely . . they are still here with me . . pieces . . like the
clouds that were following me . . all around me . . they
would come so close to touch me . . I wrap the blanket
around me tighter because when they touch my skin it's
like a winter breeze that comes through the window . . cold
and icy. It's like those clouds are still here in my room. I can
almost see them hovering above my bed . . in front of
the door when it opens . . hiding the light from the hallway . . foggy . . making it dull and gray and I like that
because my eyes are only half-open and too much light isn't
good for you when you are in between sleeping and
thinking.

I can see them like ghosts . . like shadows on a photograph. I can see the prince and his horse that were there in
my dream with me . . I can see the king and I can see me in
a dress with jewelry.

But the electricity is too strong and the people from my
dream burn off like frost on the grass now in early winter . .
disappear like smoke. The prince has gone back into the
woods . . the king has gone down through holes in the
ground . . and I have gone back to being only me.

I pull the sheet over my head when the door opens.
I am awake now . . there is nothing in between now.
It is still night.

I don't have to see to know it is my mother who is coming into my room . . her smell fills the space that the clouds left empty . . smell of lavender and newspapers. I try not to pay attention to it. I try to ignore it as it gets stronger . . as she gets closer . . because if I let myself breathe it I will forget that I'm mad at her . . I will remember only that I feel safe around the scent of lavender and newsprint.

–Lacie? Are you awake sweetie?– and it is different from hearing when you are under the covers . . when your head is turned away and you do not know how far away her voice is coming from. The words don't seem to touch my ears but come inside me from everywhere and send shivers through me.

I can feel her hesitate . . I don't have to see to feel it . . feel her arm reach out but stopping just before touching my shoulder . . pulling back.

I don't want her to. I know I kept my fingers crossed under the blanket hoping she would go away . . I know it is what I wished for but when she pulls her hand away I feel my heart break.

I feel so bad for giving her such a hard time the last few days . . feel so bad for hating her . . for saying I hated her to Benji. I don't hate her . . I just want her to change.

—I thought maybe you'd be waiting up for me today.— She is sitting on the side of my bed now . . facing away from me the same as I am facing away from her. *—I don't know why I thought that. I just had a feeling.—* Her voice sounds so tired and sad that I have to fight to keep myself from jumping up and hugging her the way Malky would.

I haven't waited up for her since she did that to me . . since she made me feel so dumb when she knew it was hard enough that day. She said she was sorry . . said it more than once but somehow it never felt like enough. I don't know what I wanted her to do though . . it's not like she could go back and make things happen in a way that is different.

—I miss you waiting up for me.— She is getting up and getting ready to leave until I sit up . . pushing the covers away from my face.

–*I thought you were always telling me not to.*– I don't want it to but I know my voice comes out sounding snotty . . and I guess I'm still mad at her . . madder than I thought when she was sitting near me.

She comes back toward me . . blocking the light behind her so that I cannot see her face . . something like the clouds in my dream and I don't want her to come too close . . wishing for a second that I hadn't said anything and just let her go away.

It is too late though . . too late even to pretend that I'm too tired to talk.

She pulls her knee onto the bed. I pull the covers up to my shoulders so that she cannot see anything except my face which I keep turned away from her so that I don't have to see her caring . . because I'm not ready to forgive her just yet.

–*I used to wait up for your father. He used to say the same thing to me . . he didn't want me to stay up either but I did. I know he liked that I did.*– I bite my lower lip . . I don't want to talk about him . . not when it's dark . . not now. She can tell . . she can always tell . . –*The point is . . sometimes we say things but we really mean the opposite.*–

130

–I wish you wouldn't . . say things you don't mean.– I say as quiet as I can and she smiles but it is a smile that is really like a frown.

We stay quiet for a long time . . seems like a long time . . seems like days and days that we stay quiet . . only the sound of things outside my window . . only the sound of us breathing.

–Did your brother eat?–
I don't answer.
I'm not going back to pretending . . I'm not going to let her go back so easily.

–I'm not a little kid. You can't treat me like one.– I'm barely able to get the words out before they choke me . . before they would turn into sounds instead of syllables . . and I barely turn away before she is able to see the redness around my eyes.

She answers by putting her hand on my knee . . holding on and I realize how much I've missed her the last few days . . how much I've missed the way she used to be before everything in our family was broken . . and I realize how much I've missed my dad too . . how much he always made things better . . how he could laugh the way my mom can't . . and I guess I've been wanting her to be both and I never should have. It's not fair.

–I know sweetie. I know.– Her eyes are red too when she reaches over . . when she puts her arms around me and holds me close to her so that I can cry without making any noise.

I can't stop thinking about everything that is wrong and wondering why it has to happen to me . . why our house can't be as pretty and perfect on the inside as it is on the outside . . why I can't be more like the toy houses my father used to give to me . . pretty on the outside and empty on the inside . . like most of the other kids at school. Why do I have to care so much about things? . . why can't I just hate her the way Jenna and Mandy hate their moms? . . and it makes me cry . . thinking about all of this . . about how I can't just be normal the way everyone else is . . why I have to cry like my little brother to make it not hurt so much.

My mother's hand on the back of my head . . my hands covering my mouth. I make myself stop . . make myself hold it in.

Mom reaches across me and switches the lamp on beside my bed . . a soft yellow glow off the pink walls . .

halos around our eyes from tears and she uses her sleeves to wipe away the streaks on my chin. I still won't look at her though . . still afraid to see her clearly . . scared of what thoughts it will make for me to look at her. I sniff everything back up inside me and look away out the window at the tree branches that scrape the glass like the fingernails of the wind.

I see her looking around . . searching . . seeing things like a mother again . . checking up. She hasn't been in my room in so long . . she is noticing things . . the houses moved down from the shelves . . the way I've started keeping my clothes more on the floor than put away . . the way I have my stuffed animals in the corner instead of my bed so that Jenna won't tease me about them so much . . noticing everything as if recording a list of things and places will make up for not being here to live through the last however long it's been.

Then her eyes stop . . something on the floor and my heart stops even though I don't know what it could be . . but the way her eyes freeze. I put my fingers in my mouth . . knowing it must be something I never wanted her to see . . thinking of things that I keep secret in my room . . the notebooks under my bed . . the nightgown I stole from her room . . the black one that shows through . . keeping

133

my fingers crossed even inside my mouth and hoping it's nothing.

I feel like I lose a million pounds when she smiles . . her hand reaching down and in the soft light I notice that her hands don't look as old as they usually do . . knowing that in the morning they will again.

She is holding a picture I drew . . *–Is this him?–* she asks. It's not the best of him I've done . . his eyes the wrong color blue . . his hands not really the right shape . . but yes it's him.

I nod that it's him and hope she doesn't make any comments . . hope she doesn't try to make it sound like a silly crush . . hope she doesn't try to be my friend and say that he looks cute. But that is not my mother . . she is not like those mothers in any way and I guess I forgot the good things about her being the way she is.

–You really like him. Don't you?–

–Mmm-hmmm– still with my fingers holding my tongue still . . holding in how much I really like him . . how he can make me feel the way we are supposed to feel . . how he can make me forget the things that hurt when I'm with him and that's all I ever want.

She doesn't say anything . . only stands up from my bed and tucks me in the way she hasn't since I was 10 . . walking over to my dresser to place the picture carefully on top . . –*I love you . . so much and I don't . . I just don't want you to ever get hurt.*–

But everything already hurts . . how could he do anything worse than has already happened to me? And he wouldn't anyway . . he loves me . . he would never . . he wouldn't hurt me the way our father did . . the way he hurt her . . the way his mother is hurting him . . he wouldn't ever.

–*I'm going to let go on this one*– she says . . says that I'm right that I'm not a little kid . . that I'm old enough to feel the way I do and that she won't try to stop me. –*Just promise me Lacie . . promise you'll talk more to me about these things? Promise you'll be careful.*–

–*I promise Mom*– and then I yawn and she kisses my head before turning the light out. And as she closes the door I wonder if it is a promise I will keep.

day 53

day 53

Jenna is pulling at my arm . . I'm pretending to be mad at her for teasing me . . at least she thinks I'm pretending . . really I am mad at her. I can only show it by pretending to be . . by pouting and by walking away from her. But I've carried on too long and I think she is starting to tell that I'm not so much pretending.

–*Don't be so gay it was just a stupid joke*– she says to me. I try pulling my arm away but she grabs tighter until her fingernails dig into my skin . . her face looks like she's only playing but she's digging tighter and tighter until I stop fighting her and we both stop pretending to be angry and actually are.

–*It wasn't funny*– I say.

–It *wasn't funny It wasn't funny*– Jenna and Kara say together . . making their voices sound whiny like my voice . . tossing their heads to the side the way I did . . then putting their fingers up to their mouths like I am now. They are laughing like best friends and it is like I'm a million miles away and the me who is standing in front of them is only like an animal in the zoo for them to make fun of.

I wish I were invisible . . I wish the entire world were invisible and we never had to see anyone ever in our whole lives.

Jenna is bored with me . . it's like that when her eyes go dull. She's bored with me being mad at her . . bored with the way I'm acting toward her . . the way I haven't warmed up to her yet and so she is going to make it worse. That is what she always does. That is why I usually only try to pretend to be mad at her . . because she will always try to win if she thinks we are fighting.

–*Eww gross*– she says . . taking her fingers away from her mouth and wiping them off on her shirt . . wiping the saliva off the corner of her mouth . . –*SEE! That's what I mean . . it's not my fault you do so many weird things!*–

My mouth won't move to speak . . and I guess if I were more normal I would say something mean back at her . . I would stand up for myself or try to at least make her feel just as bad. I could. I know things about her . . her secrets . . but I don't tell. I can't tell. She knows I can't tell and that is what makes her strong and makes me weak.

Her eyes turn away from me . . turn to Kara where they stay . . Jenna's blue eyes so bright that they make Kara's seem lighter . . make the green of her eyes glow like a cat's . . like the cats that are hung up in trees with their bellies shot open and I know she's afraid of Jenna . . I know through her smile that really she is just hoping Jenna stays with picking on me . . trying to do all the right things to keep on her good side.

I don't want to be on her good side. Not after what she did . . the way she was teasing me last period in gym class. When I looked over at her I didn't know at first that it was me she was teasing . . I only heard the other girls laughing . . saw Jenna pointing at something and I didn't know what it was so I smiled too and then they laughed harder. That's how I knew it was me . . that she was pointing at me and looked down to see that my underwear had come down a little when I was changing into my gym clothes.

I know Kara is remembering it all too . . knowing that next time it could be her . . seeing the girls laugh at her and that is why she keeps smiling . . her whole body tight and nervous and ready to do whatever Jenna does . . breathing out so much easier when Jenna turns back to me.

I'm so afraid of the way Jenna is looking at me. If I were to draw her I'd draw her like a giant insect with long claws . . snarling and hungry . . I'd draw her with quick angry lines from the pencil . . striking the paper so hard with the point that there would be tiny tears in the drawing.

I make the mistake of turning away from her . . of not just letting it go but giving her another reason to tease me.

—Hey Lacie— she says. I turn around again to see her hand moving down her chest . . pausing to hold herself there the way Avery held her . . moving her hand down her stomach and reaching for the end of her shirt . . *—You gonna give us another peep show?—* pulling her shirt up so that I can see her belly button.

A boy walks by behind me . . his eyes getting bigger each inch Jenna's hand goes up.

It's her who wants to . . I wasn't doing anything. It's her who was watching me in the first place. She knows how shy I get . . I wish she wouldn't.

But she doesn't stop. She lifts her hand one more inch and then another and now there are four boys watching with their eyes like puppy eyes . . mouths open . . staring at her like something they've never seen except in magazines . . watching like watching the sun exploding. Her eyes are shining at them . . lifting one more inch until they see the white of her bra and then she drops her shirt back down and gives them the middle finger . . winks at them when they groan and walk away.

I'm going to walk away too.
I won't let her do this to me.
I won't let her make me feel bad about myself.

I take five steps when I feel her fingers slip in between mine as I start walking away . . feel her palm against mine and feel how warm she is . . how soft . . like nothing I've felt from her all day.

I stop.
I won't turn around though.

Her hand squeezes mine tighter. I close my eyes. I think to myself if I were blind I would almost have thought it was Benji's hand . . the way she is holding mine the same as he does . . the way our fingerprints rub together . . the way we

are siamese . . the way her touch can make me forget everything that is making the knots in my stomach . . making me
forget everything I hate about her and only remember the
way I need her like I have since 4th grade.

–*Come on Lacie . . I'm sorry. I'm only kidding.*– Her
mouth so close behind my ear . . her voice like a little
breeze . . her other hand coming up to push the curls away
from my eyes so that she can see me. –*Still friends. Right?*–
I nod . . still friends.

*   *   *

–*No I don't get it*– he says . . shaking his head and I want
him to stop . . I don't want him to be mad . . I don't want to
talk anymore or explain anymore because I can't.

I hold on to his hands but he doesn't hold mine back . .
keeping his arms stiff at his sides . . –*She's my best friend*– I
say for the third time . . hoping that it is enough to explain
why I can't go with him today after school . . why I'm going

to my house with Jenna instead of him . . hoping that holding his hands is enough to explain because holding hands can say more than words sometimes.

–*I don't know why she's your best friend. All she does is make you feel bad so she feels better about herself.*– His face is redder than normal . . his eyes with a heat around them.

He's making me do this . . making it a choice and I don't want it to be a choice. –*That's not true*– I tell him but he only rolls his eyes.

It's just today . . just one day . . the only day she's asked to come over in so long. Benji says that's only because Avery has to go to his grandmother's . . that she would never want to if it wasn't for that. He's not trying to be mean . . I know he's only saying what it looks like . . but I want him to stop . . –*please*– . . it's not like it looks . . she's still my best friend.

–*She's mean*– he says and that's when I let go of him . . that's when everything inside me twists up so tight that it hurts. But just when it feels like I can't take it anymore he puts his hands on my shoulders . . –*Sorry*– he says. –*I'm sorry. I just want to see you. That's all.*–

–*Tomorrow. Okay?*– Tomorrow I will spend the entire afternoon with him . . tomorrow will be like yesterday and the day before . . tomorrow will be only for us.

–*Yeah . . okay*– he says and I lift up on my tiptoes and place my lips on his mouth and he kisses me back weakly . . lets go of my shoulders and separates from me . . walks away slowly and doesn't turn around to see me with my hand by my face ready to wave at him if he were to look back at me.

He doesn't . . not until he turns into the next hall . . looks back quickly and I wave my hand so fast my bones might snap off at the wrist and he waves back to me . . smiles at me but he can't hide everything behind his smile . . can't hide that he is upset. Then he is gone and I stand alone in the middle of people passing.

I listen to the sound of their shoes on the linoleum . . the sneakers squeaking and the parts of conversations that come and go. So many kids walking past . . not noticing me . . and I feel like a child who has lost her parents . . who is waiting for them to come back and find her.

–*What was his problem?*– Her voice startles me . . so close and I didn't hear her approaching with all the other sounds of people walking. Her face says everything . . says how much she hates him . . about as much as he hates her and I feel two parts of me torn down the middle . . the part that is standing here with her and the other part that walked down the hallway with him and is gone from me for right now.

–*You ready?*– she says and I nod to her . . feeling lost and happy that she is here to lead me away.

The whole world seems to be placed in a way to make it easier to hide . . the way the houses are tucked into neat little pockets of tall maple trees . . the way the rooms are set off in different corners inside with doors and walls to close off everything else. They are all trying to make you hide the way you feel . . to keep it tucked away in those rooms . . to keep it tucked inside you away from anyone who may be in there with you.

Jenna and I are doing that . . talking but not saying anything.

She is lying on my bed . . her socks on my pillow . . her elbows holding her up so she can flip through the magazine she has with her. I wonder if she notices it too . . that we are not really talking to each other . . that I'm sitting over at my desk but I might as well be sitting in the next town or the next state.

I wonder if she is thinking about Avery . . about the way his hand feels on her stomach . . if she's thinking about him as much as I'm thinking about Benji. Maybe she's not thinking about anything though . . just the pictures in the magazine. She's always saying I think too much . . and I wonder how it's possible not to . . if that's something that she can teach me.

–*It's too bad your hair doesn't look like this*– she says . . pointing to a photograph of a girl wearing a heavy brown sweater and smiling so that you might want to buy it.

I look at the girl's hair . . a little longer than mine . . the curls not so tight . . the sweater the same color and everything about her is perfect.

–*It would be prettier if it wasn't so curly*– . . running her hand through her own perfectly straight hair. She doesn't mean anything by it. I know she doesn't but that doesn't stop me from looking in the mirror . . from feeling that I'm not as pretty as I should be.

I pull at a few strands of my hair . . pull them until they are straight. Still the same me.

I look out the window at the sky.
The sky looks like dirty newspaper . . gray and old.

It's almost time for my mom to call to say she's going to be late . . almost time for Jenna's mom to call to say Jenna is going to be late if she doesn't leave soon.

I'm watching the trees outside . . so skinny in the winter that they dance in the wind. The tree branches scratch at the window . . their trunks bending in the wind and I am like those trees . . their branches like the little bones that run through me. Anything strong could break them . . snap them off one by one until they disappear. And we are all just hoping that we are strong enough to last through the winter . . me and the trees.

–I'm bored– Jenna says as she sits up on the bed and folds the magazine closed . . pushing back to lean against the wall . . to lean against my pillow that will smell like her tonight when I go to sleep . . moving aside the sweater she has taken off to make room for me.

It scares me sometimes that she has to do so little to get

me to do what she wants. She only had to yawn and push aside a few things to get me to put down the pencil in my hand and walk over to the bed. Her eyes pulling me closer . . glowing blue the way the stars do in a purple sky . . watching the way I walk . . the way my legs cross in front of each other and watching how I keep my arms still at my side and keep them away from my face like she showed me to. I'm trying to be perfect for her . . I'm trying to be the way she wants me to be . . the way that other girls in school are. I'm trying.

Jenna smiles and it makes me feel like I only exist for her . . I only exist to make her happy or angry and everything else doesn't matter . . not to her.

I sit down by her feet and wait for her to talk. I fold my hands in front of me . . waiting for her to tell me what she wants me to do next.

Jenna puts her feet in my lap. Her socks are stained on the bottom from the leather of her shoes. I look down at them . . following from her feet to her knees that are bent slightly and then up to her stomach and her arms that stretch to rest behind her head. I let the heels of her feet rest in the palms of my hands and hold them the way I would hold anything that was delicate or made from porcelain.

151

Benji holds me that way . . his hands careful with me. I open my mouth to tell her . . to whisper to her what it feels like when he touches my face or when he is pressed up against me on the ground in that old house where we lie together.

I bite my lip before anything slips out.

We never talk about him. Jenna never wants to hear about him. If I bring him up she only rolls her eyes . . says it doesn't mean anything . . that all we've done is kissed and that she knows what *that* feels like. I don't have to tell her what that is like and so I don't have to tell her anything. Last time I tried to tell her anything she said I could talk about him once he's seen me naked . . then she turned to Mandy and they laughed . . whispered secrets to each other about what it is like to be naked with a boy and I turned red and that made them laugh harder.

–*You're such a prude*– Mandy said and I felt like crying . . I didn't though . . I held it in . . I'm good at holding it in . . better than before. Jenna would have said I was only being gay and maybe she would have been right . . I don't know. It shouldn't bother me so much . . it's only words . . *sticks and stones may break my bones* . . but it's easier to say that when you're little . . when you can actually believe it's true.

I only even smiled at Benji that first time because I wanted to fit in . . I wanted to be like Mandy and Kara . . the way they let boys talk to them like they're special . . the way they let them tease them and touch them. I only wanted to be more normal so that Jenna and I would be best friends again . . so that she wouldn't need to tell them things she didn't tell me. I only ever talked to Benji for her. But it's like I can never keep up . . I can never go fast enough for her and every day there is more space between us.

–OWW! Stop it! What are you doing?– I look down and see that I'm digging my fingers into her foot . . so hard that she is trying to pull her leg away but can't.

I let go suddenly . . I didn't know . . I was lost in all my thinking and I didn't know.

–What did you do that for?– . . looking away from me . . sitting up so that she can reach down and rub her ankle. Her fingers moving in my lap like tiny spiders.

–I'm sorry– I say but I can see the lines around her eyes . . can hear the anger in the way she breathes. I can smell her shampoo . . flowers and soap and knowing that it will stay there on my pillow for me to think of her when she

is gone. –*I'm sorry*– I say again and Jenna doesn't look at me.

I don't want to feel so separate from her anymore. I don't want to feel like two houses set apart by trees and lawns. I want to feel close to her like the way we used to be when we didn't know any better. Why can't it be like that? Like the first time she ever came to my room . . I remember every way she moved her hands . . the blue dress she wore with white-and-pink sneakers . . the way her mouth opened like it was Christmas morning when she ran her small fingers over the houses my father had given me . . and I remember which one she picked to pretend was her house . . the one she would get married in and live in but we never mentioned any boys back then.

I wonder if she remembers . . even though she thinks it's babyish to talk about it . . I wonder if she remembers anyway.

Her hand is still in my lap and I wrap my fingers around hers the way she did with me in the hallway at school today. She lifts her chin and brushes her hair from her face and I wonder if she can remember everything I want her to just by looking in my eyes. Maybe if I lean closer . . if our eyes almost touch and then maybe. Maybe she will remember me . . the white shirt with the rainbow that I wore that first day she was in here . . the tent we built out of my blankets and how we hid in there with all my stuffed animals and pretended we were the only people in the world.

She's starting to remember . . all the secrets that we have are starting to show in her eyes . . like blue sparks of electricity . . closer.

I know she is remembering when I feel her put her hand on me . . resting there the way I saw Avery's resting on her . . my heart races and I wonder if she can feel it in her fingers . . my whole body shivers the way it does when I'm alone with myself and Jenna smiles when she feels me shake because she remembers . . remembers the time after my dad died . . when she slept over and I started crying until she put her arms around me . . until she kissed me.

I thought she forgot our biggest secret . . the one we never talk about . . the one that feels almost more like a dream that I'm not sure ever happened. My first kiss.

This time I know it's not a dream . . the sun is still fading in the sky and I can hear cars driving along the highway out behind our house. I know it's real this time when I lean closer into her so that our breath meets.

I know that it's real but I don't feel real. I don't feel anything but the way our lips feel pressed against each other. I don't feel my legs go weak the way they do when Benji kisses me . . I don't feel the stars in my head or the swirling clouds the way I do when he pushes his tongue inside my mouth. It feels different with Jenna . . feels safer because we are not in love . . feels like a memory and not at all like something that is happening right now.

–*What are you guys doing?*– coming from my bedroom door . . each syllable like an explosion inside me.

I pull away from her . . see him hugging the door frame . . hiding his face halfway behind the wall. I wonder how long he's been there and how much he saw. –*Nothing. Go away!*– I shout . . telling him to go back to his room but it's too late. Hoping inside that he won't tell. Hoping he won't because when he told about Benji I didn't talk to him for three days.

Jenna pushes away from me and I turn away from Malky to look at her. –*Gross!*– She wipes at her mouth . . I reach up for her and she slaps my hand away and I don't know what I've done. –*I'm leaving*– she says and picks her sweater off the bed . . she doesn't bother to get the magazine and I stutter trying to say something to make her stay.

It was her though! It was her that leaned into me. Wasn't it her that put her hand on me and made me remember? I didn't do anything.

–Jenna wait– . . but she doesn't even turn around as she pushes by Malky through the door. I hear her running . . taking two steps at a time down the stairs. I get up and run to the bedroom door . . shout her name again but she picks up her shoes and reaches for the front door without putting them on. I'm only halfway down the stairs when she turns around . . black streaks of eye makeup on her cheeks like demons . . I open my mouth to say something and she opens hers to say something back but we both hold it in instead.

I let myself slide down the wall as the door closes . . sitting on the stairs and seeing her legs through the windows at the top of the door as she walks down the sidewalk.

Everything inside me is so confused that I can't think . . so many thoughts twisted up inside me like sunbeams tied up in knots burning through my skin. I don't know why I make everyone run away from me. I don't know what I do wrong that everyone wants to leave me alone . . my dad and my mom . . Jenna . . the way Benji walked away from me today and I know that one day he'll walk away forever the same way.

–*What's the matter?*– Malky asks . . coming down the stairs toward me . . but slowly. Even he doesn't want to get too close to me.

–*What were you doing?*– and I only shake my head so that he knows not to ask any more questions.

*   *   *

I'm waiting in the dark for the phone to ring. I won't turn on the lights and I won't turn on the television. The noise makes me frightened . . the sound of voices. I like the silence and the dark when I'm waiting.

I called her house two times.

I want to tell her so many things . . I want to say I'm sorry. I want to say that I didn't do anything and that I don't want her to be mad at me. I want to promise her I won't tell anyone just like we've always promised. I want to make sure it's a secret. I want to make sure we are still friends because even if she's mean to me sometimes she's still my only friend.

I know she's home . . I can tell in her mother's voice that she's lying when I call . . when she says Jenna isn't home. I wonder what she told her mom about me that makes it so easy for her to lie.

I'm waiting for him to call too.

I'm waiting to hear his voice through the wires that stretch out over the streets and into my living room. When I hear his voice it won't matter about her anymore . . he can make me forget about her for a little bit if he calls. He promised he would.

Until they call I will feel empty inside. I need them both to make me feel whole. Maybe I need them too much but I can't make myself stop needing.

I keep my fingers crossed beneath the blanket . . keep my other hand in my mouth and bring my knees up to my stomach to make myself as small as possible on the sofa. Everything is so quiet without the television on. I can hear Malky toss and turn in his bed above the ceiling. I can still hear him promising not to tell my mom when he saw me crying.

In the shadows I can see them . . crawling inside the

wallpaper. Angels and demons. Their eyes a little darker than the shadows . . watching me . . always watching me but neither ever seem to want to get close enough. Maybe now they will . . maybe now that everyone has left me . . that nobody wants me . . maybe now they will come to take me away like they took my dad away . . crawling down the walls and beneath carpet . . moving like insects move under the ground and I spread my arms and legs out so that they can come inside me if they want . . so that they can make me into a ghost if they want and that way I never have to feel anything again.

If I should die before I wake . . and the headlights of a passing car pass over me on the sofa . . the blanket thrown to the floor and I take my hand away from my face . . *If I should die before I wake I hope I don't come back again* . .

The silence is shattered when the phone rings. The demons and the angels retreat when the phone rings twice and I almost faint even though I was waiting for it.

I want it to be him.

All this time in the dark I wasn't sure who I wanted it to be. But I want it to be him.

My hand is shaking when I pick up the phone and put it to my ear . . my voice is too quiet and I have to clear my throat before I say *—hello—* and then squeeze my fingers crossed so tight that my bones may break like twigs snapping under sneakers.

—Lacie?— and I can feel my heart being torn apart like demon claws ripping and grabbing inside me *—I'm going to be a little longer tonight.—*

I nod because I can't find words anywhere to say.

—Everything okay?—

I make some noise with my mouth that shows that it is.

—Were you able to do the laundry?—

I shake my head . . I wasn't able to do anything.

—If you could put it in the washer I'll switch it to the dryer when I get home. Okay?—

—Okay.—

—Love you— and then her voice trails away to the sound

of dishes being piled on top of each other and forks scraping plates and tired voices talking about how much farther they need to drive to get to where they are going before they can rest.

I put the phone down.

I know that it will not ring again.

I don't feel anything as I climb the stairs. I don't feel anything as I open the closet door and reach my hands deep into the hamper to lift out a pile of dirty clothes and sheets.

day 64

I think there has never been so much sunshine . . pouring through the glass hallways of my school so I'm blinded when I turn from the dark hallway that has no windows.

It must be because of the snow . . so much of it that it feels like it could fill an ocean if you scooped it all up in your hands and moved it handful by handful. But the clouds have gone now . . have all broken apart and fallen in tiny flakes and now they lie on the ground tossing the sunbeams back up at the sky . . making it so it's like walking through heaven when I walk through the hallway . . the clouds beneath me as snow and the sun soaks my arms so that it is like walking through the sky with my eyes slightly closed.

Sometimes you can feel on the inside the way it looks on the outside . . the way the sun can make you smile . .

165

the way the whole world seems to come from inside you and color everything all the right colors and always within the lines.

Sometimes you can be tricked into feeling that way . . the way the light is . . the way my skin feels warm even with the wind striking cold against the glass on the other side.

It almost works.
I almost believe I feel that way.

But sunshine is not at all how I feel. I felt more like me when the sky was somewhere unseen above the gray clouds . . when the clouds were falling in tiny broken pieces across the ground and one by one the colored leaves were covered up to disappear forever.

That's how I feel inside. That's how I feel when Benji is not near me . . when he's not so close that I can touch his hand or his hair or even the corner of his sleeve.

He hasn't been in school today or yesterday.

I haven't heard his voice because every time I call a computer tells me the telephone line has been disconnected.

I don't know if I can take another day. I don't know if I can keep my fingers crossed that long without knowing if my wishing even works. I worry that if I don't see him soon I will forget everything about him . . that he will fade like pictures fade in old photographs . . that if I go too long without seeing him that he will forget why he likes me . . that he'll remember why no one else does.

Kara told me not to worry . . that it was nothing to worry about. –*People get sick all the time Lacie. It's no big deal.*– I wanted to tell her about how it's different . . when someone is completely inside you so that every part of you is attached to every part of them . . it is a big deal . . it is something to worry about. But she didn't really want to know . . she only said it so that I would stop sulking . . so that I would take my fingers out of my mouth and stop embarrassing her in study hall.

She wouldn't have even said that much if there was anyone else she knew in there . . someone cooler . . someone she could talk to instead of me. She would have gotten out of her seat and walked over to them. She could have talked to them about trying out for the swim team . . they could have listened to her talk and they could have told her how good she was and then she wouldn't have to say anything to cheer me up. She wouldn't have had to teach me that things like swim tryouts are more important than boys that live in trailer parks on the edge of town.

Maybe he already doesn't like me.
Maybe he sees me the way everyone else does now.

And the more I think about him the more my stomach feels sick thinking about all the things he might think. And the more my stomach feels sick the more I need to see him because I know if I see him it can be different because I can fix anything that is wrong with me . . for him I can.

I wish it would start snowing again.
I wish the sun would hide until everything is okay again.

I have to stop walking when I feel like I'm going to vomit . . I look away from the windows because the sunshine is making it worse . . I look down at my feet because the kids passing by me make me dizzy . . the sound of their voices and the sound of their sneakers and the clicking of the zippers on their backpacks as they walk.

Deep breaths.
Put my fingers on my lips to cover them.
A few steps more into the shadows again.

I'm worrying too much. I'm worrying too much about Benji and I'm worrying too much about what I have to do now to see him . . about asking her . . asking Jenna if she would ask Avery to drive me to his house because I don't know exactly where he lives to be able to walk there in the snow.

I try to tell myself that it won't be so bad . . that she won't say anything because more than me she doesn't want anyone to know.

She pretends like nothing happened . . not that day and not any day . . pretending like we were never really that much of best friends . . pretending like I'm no more than Mandy or the girl she met in Geometry this year. It hurts too much to watch her pretend. It has been better to avoid her. It doesn't hurt so much that way . . that way I can pretend that she will get over it . . that she will forgive me for whatever I did wrong.

Today I will though . . I have to . . I will talk to her because I cannot pretend the same way with Benji.

Jenna doesn't see me until Avery points at me with his eyes . . his lips move . . *–There's Lacie–* he says to her and I can see her shoulders tense up beneath her sweater. I keep my fingers crossed to keep from saying the wrong things . . trying to practice in my head what I'm going to say . . practice over and over so that I don't say the wrong thing because no matter what I have to see him . . I have to get them to drive me.

–Hi– she says . . putting her hands on her hips and blowing the hair away from her face. I hold the strap of my backpack and hug it to my chest . . take my other hand from my pocket and uncross my fingers . . wave shyly and make sure not to look her in the eye.

I turn to look up at Avery . . everything about me feels so small when he raises his eyebrows waiting for me to speak. I want to run away so badly . . my feet want to keep running and running until they are frozen in the snow . . until I fall down and my fingers and nose turn pink with frost and the clouds start breaking apart again to cover me where no one will ever find me.

–What do you want Lacie?– Jenna snaps at me . . saying the words the way she does when she is trying to sound older . . the way she says everything when Avery is around so that he will see how mature she is . . so that he won't think she was ever like me . . that she was ever as dumb as me standing here with my arms folded in front of me . . too scared to do anything but stand here like a statue that people make fun of when they pass.

–*Umm* . . – but the way she is looking at me makes me go quiet. I know when she looks at me now she only sees me on the stairs in my house . . she only sees herself on the stairs in my house. And what if she never sees anything else again? What if she will hate me forever the way she hates me today and yesterday and the days before that? And she makes me forget the words I practiced . . makes me forget everything but her . . the same as she always does and we stand staring at each other like there are no other people on earth.

–*Hey by the way Lacie . . have you spoken to Dogboy at all?*– . . his voice like a small earthquake between us . . deep and able to pull our eyes away from each other's and onto him. I shake my head quickly . . press my lips closed to keep any sounds in. –*Yeah me neither. I thought maybe you'd know what he was up to.*–

Now. I have to ask now.

Jenna is grabbing for his hand . . slipping it around hers so that it covers her hand completely and I think how small she looks standing next to him . . think about the way he was on top of her and how easily he could make her disappear.

Now. If I wait they will walk away.

Avery touches her hair and she shivers . . she moves under his arm and smiles . . smiles but her eyes are mean. She wants to prove how much she loves him . . that she is not in love with me . . but I wonder who she is proving it to?

I see them leaning away . . the quick way in which they look at each other to say it's time to go.

Now. Open your mouth.

–*Ummm . . can you? . .*– and it's worked because they stop . . wait . . and I try to pull out the words that I have rehearsed . . –*I was thinking maybe if you were going that way I mean . . that maybe can you take me to his house?*– and with the last word it feels like everything inside comes out too . . that I am only a skeleton and if they say no I will turn to dust and be swept up by the janitor with the wide broom.

–*To Dogboy's?*– and I nod . . –*No problem. I just gotta grab my coat out of my locker.*–

Jenna rolls her eyes but doesn't say anything to stop him.

I let them take three steps . . then four . . five and six before I can feel my legs again enough to walk . . to follow behind them . . walking back through the hall drowning in sunlight . . the snow so bright I close my eyes . . feeling a little bit of the sunshine inside me now . . only a little bit . . only enough to make it to Benji's house.

*   *   *

The heat hums through the vents . . blowing across the seats and over their heads and I can feel it on my lips like dry sand. The snow on the roads muffles the sounds of the tires as they pull the things in the distance closer to where we sit . . safe and warm inside the car while the world shivers outside the windows.

I'm trying to memorize everything as we pass . . the turns we make and the names of the roads . . the signs that shout out the names of stores in the shopping centers. I try to imagine what Benji thinks as he passes these places . .

wondering if he feels the same about them as I do about the ones nearer to my house . . that feeling of knowing when you are home and how sometimes it feels safe and then other times it only reminds you of all the things that are wrong there and how you wish you could turn around before getting any closer.

–Is it much farther?– Jenna asks. She hasn't tried to hide how annoyed she is . . every chance she has she turns around to glare at me . . to complain that she only has two hours before she needs to be home and that I'm taking some of them away from her.

I smile at her . . a smile that means *thank you* and *sorry* at the same time but she only ignores it.

–It's right down there– Avery says . . pointing ahead past the town park that has a man-made hill where I can already see tiny bundles of coats climbing with their sleds to race down and do it all over again.

My heart jumps when he switches on the turn signal . . beating with the ticks of the green arrow that I cannot see from where I'm sitting but that's in every car ever made so I don't need to see it to know it's there.

There are trees along the median between the two lanes of cars . . one lane going toward Benji's and the other going away. Pine trees. So pretty and perfect with the snow clinging to them like paintings of Christmas. So calm and quiet and again I'm aware of how crazy everything is inside me.

What if he isn't there?
What if he doesn't want to see me?

The sign is covered in snow but I can still read it. *Tricia Meadows*. I want to tell Avery to nevermind . . to turn around . . I can just see Benji tomorrow . . I can wait another day . . I changed my mind . . it's not too long to wait for tomorrow. But before I get to open my mouth the car slows down . . the clicking of the turn signal and the car is already leaning to the right. My whole life is in front of the windshield . . everything that will ever happen to me is starting now and I feel sick again.

–*What a dump*– Jenna says staring out the window at the yards that are littered with old cars that have no engines . . sheds with broken things that no one is ever going to fix. And the trailer homes are not spaced out the way houses are in my neighborhood. There are no trees between them . . no backyards with fences and swimming pools. There are no second floors with stairs leading up to them.

I don't know which is his . . I don't know if it's around the first turn or the second . . if it has white siding or pale blue . . but it doesn't matter because I can feel him getting closer and I wonder if he can feel me nearby. I only want to get out of this car . . to run up to the door and throw my arms around him and cry and then it doesn't matter what happens next because at least we will be together.

–It's that one– Avery says. I follow where he is looking . . a tan home . . a screen door in front of the heavy red door that keeps out the cold . . a rotten pumpkin left over from Halloween in front of the mailbox and just enough of it peeking out of the snow to know it's there.

The engine seems louder when the car comes to a stop . . the radio which I only barely heard seems louder too and the nervous feeling inside my stomach feels stronger.

Jenna opens the door and the cold rushes in to fill the car. *–Hurry up . . it's freezing!–* . . turning around in her seat to watch me go . . her eyes pink around the edges . .

pulling the front seat up giving me just enough room to crawl out behind her.

–*Thanks*– I whisper as I pull my backpack closer to me and slide my sneakers onto the frozen ground.

–*Do you want us to wait?*– Avery asks.

–NO. *Let's just go!*– Jenna says to him and I can see myself shake my head in the glass . . telling him to just go . . pushing myself out so the snow crunches beneath me. I have to pull my hand away quick so that it doesn't get caught in the door as Jenna slams it closed.

The back lights of the car show red on the snow making it look like someone has died . . the color of blood on bath-room tile . . just until Avery's foot lifts up gently and gently moves to the other pedal. The car pulls away slowly . . I stand watching it go . . watching the smoke from the exhaust pipe climb up to mix with the gray clouds that are gathering again.

I wait outside for Avery to drive out of sight . . wait until the car becomes invisible in the clouds that move in faster than I would have thought . . the snow beginning to fall around me . . gathering in the curls sticking out from the bottom of my wool cap . . falling onto the snow that's already fallen . . so many inches that it seeps into my socks and soaks my feet and that is when I walk up to the door and knock.

It opens right away.

I wonder how long he was watching me through the window . . knowing he was watching me and finding the words frozen to my lips.

Benji keeps his hair hanging in his face . . he's hoping I don't notice that he's been crying. I look away to make it easier for him . . I look away so he doesn't have to hide.

I've never seen a boy cry . . never one that was older than Malky . . never one that wasn't little. I know that they do . . they must . . it's only that I've never seen them and I'm surprised that it's the same as when I cry. I don't know why I thought it would be different . . sadness is the same for both of us. The only difference is that he doesn't make any sound . . he doesn't change his expression . . only lets the tears go out the side of his eyes and then quickly wipes them away like I do.

I thought I would know what to do when I got here . . that if I could only get here then I would know. But I don't.

I don't know if I should hold him the way my mother holds me . . I don't know if I should kiss his eyes the way girls do on television . . if I should make promises I can't keep or if what I'm doing is the only thing that can be done . . if sitting here looking away is the best that I can do.

—Sorry— he says . . wiping one more time . . sniffing once to show that he's stopped . . pushing his hair from his face to let me know that he's stopped for good . . that it's okay if I look at him now. *—It's stupid—* he says and I don't say anything because he hasn't told me the sad things yet.

I don't know why he was crying . . I don't know what he thinks is stupid. He hasn't said anything to me since I got here . . only *—hi—* when he opened the door and then stepped aside. I was too cold to even say that . . I was too cold to throw my arms around him and he was too distant . . standing right there but his eyes were miles away and so I just followed behind him . . my coat and shoes still on . . following him through the kitchen and into his room.

My feet are wet inside my shoes and I move my toes around to get them warm. I can feel the warmth from the kerosene heater in the corner . . not like the warmth from a fire . . more like the warmth from a stove.

–Look I'm sorry– he says again . . this time his hand moves along the sheets . . reaching for my hand but still not looking and I put my hand in his to make it easier. And he shakes his head to shake away the things that made him sad . . trying to hide it back inside him and make it secret again.

–You were crying– I say.

–Yeah– he says and tries to smile . . gives a short laugh and then wipes his eyes again. I won't ask him why. Secrets can only be told when you want to tell them.

The snow is falling harder than before . . falling in front of the window like static on the television screen when the cable goes out. I can smell the snow through the window . . mixing in with the smell of Benji's room that is like the smell of his clothes . . the smell of sleep and old stuffed animals even though I don't see any. I only see piles of old clothes . . pieces from old board games and pictures taped to the wall . . pictures from magazines of people whose names I don't know but who I know were in bands back when pictures were taken in black and white. I don't want to ask who they are . . I don't want to sound stupid.

–They didn't want to come in?– he asks me . . pretending to be okay . . pretending that something isn't wrong inside and I'll pretend along with him . . I'll pretend for him.

–No. They had to go . . somewhere.– I don't know if they ever said where they had to go . . I keep thinking about what Jenna said about this being a dump and I know she would never come inside. He knows too though. I don't have to tell him for him to know. He knows from my eyes . . he knows from having lived here his whole life.

–Yeah somewhere– he says and looks away because I shouldn't have said anything. *–I didn't mean that–* he says and his hand moves up my arm . . *–It's just that he never–* . . then he stops and looks toward the window at the falling snow before looking back at me. *–I missed you.–*

I smile.
He smiles and I know everything is okay.

I know that nothing has changed between us . . that all the worrying I've done is stupid because he loves me . . his smile says that he loves me even more than if he said the words. Then finally he puts his arms around me . . and it is exactly like I imagined the whole way over here . . lying on his bed . . my coat still zipped up and my hands still like two ice blocks at the ends of my arms but inside everything is warm and safe.

For now . . while his mom is asleep and we are alone.

*　　*　　*

–*I HATE HER!*– he screams . . clenching his fists and his teeth grinding the way starved dogs do and I can see maybe where his nickname comes from even if it is from some old movie . . growling his words out and in the cold air I can see them in the frost that escapes his mouth.

He didn't wait until we were far enough away and I'm sure she can hear him through the thin walls of their home . . her face watching from the little window over the sink where she is only piling more dirty dishes on top of others and not trying to wash them . . watching us with her long red eyes that drag on the corners of her face.

I know she can hear him.
But I know she doesn't care.

–*It's okay. I don't mind.*– I don't mind walking back through the snow to my house . . it might take a long time but it is still early enough. And I don't mind saying that it doesn't bother me if that will make him less mad. It would have been strange to ride in a car with her anyway. My mother's home and I don't have to rush and I'm sure she will drive him back . . I'm sure she would never make him walk so far back in the snow that is still falling but only slightly.

She would never say what his mom said . . when he woke her up from her nap . . when he said –*Mom this is Lacie. Will you drive her home?*– and I stood there with my hands folded feeling small and scared in the dark room where his mom lay with empty bottles beside the bed.

–*Why?*– she said. –*She's not my kid.*–

He whispered something to her and in the dark I couldn't see his lips move . . I only heard the sound of the air passing through his teeth and thought how much I wished he wouldn't say whatever he was saying. That's when she threw the blanket off her . . throwing her arm back so violently I thought she was trying to hit him.

I was frightened when she stood up . . the way her hair

was pushed aside this way and that way and the way her eyes looked like they had never been closed in a hundred years. It startled me when she walked toward me . . I didn't mean anything when I raised my hands to cover my face . . I was startled . . that's all.

She laughed as she passed by me . . brushing up against me . . –*I'm not going to hit you honey*– . . tossing her head back the way Jenna does when she is teasing me . . walking like women walk when they try to be younger . . her legs brushing against each other as she passed . . nothing on but a long t-shirt but I was the one who felt embarrassed somehow.

I heard her in the kitchen . . shuffling her bare feet across the tiles. Benji came next to me and I asked him if we could go . . if he would walk with me. I didn't mean to be afraid . . I didn't mean to make him feel bad. I only wanted to go.

As we walk our feet leave their tracks in the snow . . mine littler than his . . softer than his. When we get to where the lawns reach the main road the snow seems to calm him . . the world covered in white . . softening his eyes as he unclenches his fists. The frost of his breath becomes more even with his steps.

–Is she always like that?– I ask him.

–Sometimes– he says.

The snowplow is like faraway thunder behind us . . scraping the road clean . . pushing aside the snow which absorbs our words. Without that I think our words would feel too real . . would hurt too much without the echo getting lost inside the soft snowflakes.

But I don't have to ask him anymore . . we don't have to talk the whole way back if he doesn't want to because I know enough to know how he feels. I know enough to know that you don't have to have a parent die to be in pain . . that sometimes having them around is more painful . . that you don't need to tell secrets in order to share them.

I know his secret now.
I know I don't have to be near him to have him with me forever.

The snowplow gets closer . . we step off the road to let it pass . . rumbling like thunder that surrounds you . . scraping against the pavement like demons scraping against glass windows . . taking the snow away like wiping the steam from the bathroom mirror and the time for secrets is over because everything is too real again . . too clean.

I smile at him the way Jenna taught me to smile at boys . . the way that she smiles to make them forget everything except her standing there in front of them. It works. All our troubles feel like they are being pushed away by the plow . . far enough away so they cannot touch us here.

Benji helps me over the snow hills on the side of the road so we can walk in the path made by the tires . . pulls me in close to him and I let him kiss me . . let him try to swallow me into him where he can keep me forever the way I will keep his secret from everyone.

day 71

I pull the covers over my head so that even the ghosts can't see me . . so even the hall light that shows under my bedroom door cannot reach me . . so that everything is dark. In the dark I can be anywhere. Under my blankets I can be anyone and do anything just as I want to do.

When the wind blows the house creaks.

My mother told me when I was younger that it was only the wind . . but I know it's the ghosts coming in through the spaces between the beams. They are coming to watch me . . crawling over the boxes in the attic marked *Baby Clothes* and *Christmas* . . and the boxes that aren't marked which are my dad's things . . going through the floor and slithering behind the wallpaper and always looking for my room.

I can feel them in here . . clear ghost eyes behind the blue flowers painted on the wallpaper. I can feel them move . . slowly . . the way my clothes slip off slowly. They become anyone I want them to become . . anyone I want watching me can be here as long as I'm under the covers with the door closed.

Yesterday they were Benji's eyes . . and the day before too. They were his eyes and that way it felt like him touching me under the sheet . . my hand felt the way his hand feels.

I pull the corners of the sheet so tight under me . . tucking them under my shoulders and my knees so that they can see the shape of me underneath like a mummy wrapped in thin paper.

I close my eyes and see trees crisscrossing the sky . . see the stars scattered like mistakes in a photograph.

I keep them shut tight and my bed is like the dirt floor in our house that will only ever be half-built like the castle I dream about. The walls of my bedroom are like the cinder blocks sunken into the ground. I will see him there tomorrow like I did today and the last five days. Tomorrow his hand will unzip my heavy coat and move beneath my clothes.

Tomorrow is too far away.

In the darkness of my bedroom it can be tomorrow already.

I have to keep my fingers in my mouth to keep from making sounds when I start to breathe quicker . . when my heart starts to beat so fast against my rib cage as my hand fights its way under the sheets pulled so tight against my skin that I can feel the pulse in my wrist.

I can feel where my body folds together . . like his hand is on fire when he touches me and my hand is his hand in the dark. Slipping inside where I don't feel so broken anymore . . remembering how clumsy it was the first time he reached inside me . . not at all like the way I do . . like someone scratching at the back of your throat . . like someone trying to take my secrets out.

In my room I don't have to be me . . I don't have to be Lacie lying in her bed . . I can be a princess lying naked in the woods. I don't have to be alone. He can be there with me . . a beautiful prince. I can be that way until I hear footsteps in the hall . . approaching my door and I panic trying to remember if I locked the door before I pulled the covers over my head. Then I am Lacie again . . I am scared and shy again . . the ghosts scream in the creaking of the house trying to get away . . taking him with them.

I pull the covers away from my face. There is no time to put my clothes on so I hold the blankets across my chest and keep my fingers crossed hoping it is not my mother whose hand is on the doorknob.

I'm blind for a second when the light floods in . . then I see Malky's hand holding the inside of the door . . see his face with his other hand near his mouth like me when I'm doing something I'm not supposed to.

–*Lacie?*– he whispers and I still haven't been able to catch my breath as he walks into my room with baby steps . . near enough to see my eyes open . . near enough to hear me breathing sharp quick breaths.

–*What do you want?*– I don't mean to be angry with him . . I know what he wants . . I know that he is still scared from this afternoon but I wish he would go into her room instead of mine. I wish he would tell her about the dead cat he found after school instead of telling me. He won't though . . made me promise not to tell her. He never tells her anything.

–Can I sleep in here with you?– . . dragging his blanket behind him like he's always done . . the one he hides from his friends who tease him about it . . calling him a baby . . and that is why he pretends to be brave standing in the shadows of my room even though I know how scared he is.

–Can't you sleep in Mom's room?– . . feeling the pile of clothes at my feet . . the sheets against my skin and not wanting him to know . . wanting him to go away so that I can be the girl in my drawings again.

He looks back to the door . . blinking at the brightness.

My mom has been better . . she has been home more . . been taking less time at work to be here. But Malky still doesn't feel comfortable around her . . not like he does around me. I don't think my mom does either . . the way she looks at him like she's looking at my dad as a boy. The way she's so careful with her words around him . . the way she never touches his face the way she touches mine.

–Okay– I say when he doesn't move from where he's standing . . when his eyes look like they are going to start crying the way they did when he came home from school today and told me about the cat hanging in the tree. *–Come*

around to this side though– and I push my clothes away with my feet and check with my hands to see that the sheet is still wrapped against me tight like a dress.

–*Close the door*– and he turns around and pushes it shut. In the last seconds of light I can see him smile before he runs around to the far side of my bed and climbs under the blanket.

When he is this close to me I can smell the sour scent of urine on him . . through the sheet I can feel that he is damp and I know that he has seen his giant tonight . . the giant from his dreams with angry teeth and its eyes sewn shut with metal wire. –*I had a bad dream*– he says like he is apologizing and I tell him I know and run my fingers through his hair the way my mom would do if I waited up for her.

When we lie here like this . . like we are siamese the way his shoulders are pressed together under my arm . . I think about how no matter what changes everything stays almost the same . . that there are only moments of forgetting everything that is wrong and sometimes the moments last longer . . but right then when you close your eyes . . when you can feel the sleep on your eyelids . . that is when you remember . . that is when you know what it means not to be perfect.

day 73

It's a hard shape to make . . the way the body moves in the wind is hard to catch with the pencil. I have to keep erasing it and starting over. The lines are so heavy from repeating them . . my fingers stained gray from smoothing out the lead on the paper to make shadows around the three figures I'm trying to copy from a book . . the lines are hard to draw . . the curve of their backs and the way the rope makes their necks long like swans'.

The librarian keeps looking at me . . pushing her glasses up on her nose and clearing her throat each time I begin to use the eraser . . narrowing her eyes at the crumbs that I brush away onto my lap . . onto the floor of the school library. I call it a library but last year they changed the name of it to *Media Center* when they put in new comput-ers and more televisions and took away most of the books because no one wanted to read them I guess. I don't mind making a mess in a *Media Center* . . there is nothing that makes it special like a library.

Some books are still here though. This one is . . the one on Joan of Arc with all the old drawings in it that I like to copy.

I've copied most of them already . . but this one I can't get right. The three dead people hanging in an open field . . the clouds so beautiful and the fields of wheat so peaceful that the bodies look like angels and that is why I copy them . . that is why I copy all the pictures from the book . . because they're beautiful and she is so beautiful. Sometimes I like to think she was like me . . the way she lived with ghosts and talked to them . . made her different. I know I'm different. But maybe I can be brave and beautiful too.

—That's really cool. You're good.— A stranger's voice beside me . . near me so close and sitting down across from me.

I cover up the picture. I fold my hands over the piece of paper and let the pencil drop. She laughs. *—That's okay—* she says. *—I didn't mean for you to stop.—*

I look at the table next to me . . to the right . . to the left . . wonder if she sat at the wrong one by mistake. It's hard to see her face . . the windows behind me lighting her like the flash on a camera. I see enough to know that I don't know her . . that I don't want to share my picture with her.

–*Who are they?*– she asks me . . pointing to the page in the book where the three bodies are hanging by their necks from ropes attached to poles . . hanging like scarecrows to frighten away entire armies . . the sun in their hair like the sun on the fur of cats hung by string on the trees in my neighborhood.

I think maybe she might be a teacher . . the way she talks . . so sure of herself . . the way she came up to me and just started talking like we've known each other our whole lives. But the sound of her voice isn't a teacher's and the t-shirt she wears over a thin sweater isn't what a teacher wears. When she leans in closer to me and I see her face . . young like me . . then I know for sure she's not a teacher.

I know who she is . . she's a sophomore like Benji but she's a year older than him . . held back . . something about her going away and then coming back is what everyone says. I don't know where she went . . just that she went away. I heard one kid say she was in jail . . but I heard another say she ran away. One girl said both of those were lies and she just went to live with her aunt for a while because she was pregnant.

I don't know which is right and I don't know if I care. I only know I don't want to pull my hands away from my picture . . that I don't really want to talk. I want to finish drawing before the period ends . . I want to get the shape of the bodies being pushed by the wind so that tomorrow I can copy the next picture . . the one of Joan of Arc at the walls of heaven . . the shape of her body like mine under the gown that's transparent like a ghost's skin.

–I didn't want to bother you . . I mean I just . . I don't know. I just thought it was a cool drawing– she says . . pushing the chair back . . angry with me maybe.

I try to smile. I don't want to be mean to her . . remembering Jenna's eyes when I was new at school . . remembering no one wanting to talk to me.

I open my mouth . . she stops . . half-standing up . . waiting for me to say something.

–Thanks.– I uncover the picture so she can see.

She smiles . . says she'll go so I can finish but makes me promise to show it to her when it's done. *–My name's Gretchen by the way–* she says and I say *–hi–* and tell her my name too. I watch her walk three tables away and start to read a book that she's brought with her.

I watch her . . the way she tucks her blond hair behind her ear like softer pieces of straw . . the way she brings her knees between her and the table so that her feet dangle above the carpet. And I know by watching her that she doesn't worry about things the way I do . . that she doesn't care so much what people think.

I look at my drawing again . . look at the one in the book . . realize that I've already finished it. I've already made the lines exactly the way they've been made in the book. I smile.

–What did she want?– and I see Jenna walking toward me with a magazine in her hand . . walking like she's in a parade . . walking for everyone to look at her and I think I will never understand how she is able to show herself like that . . how she is able to be so comfortable with how pretty she looks.

–I don't know. Nothing really– I say and look over at Gretchen who looks up from her book and smiles at me . . I feel my face go red so I quickly look away.

Jenna is looking over at her . . narrowing her eyes at me the way the librarian did. She doesn't like her . . the way she keeps looking back at her three tables away and making that face . . the one that lets me know Gretchen doesn't fit Jenna's rules for who to be and who to like . . anyone who isn't perfect isn't worth talking to.

Her rules don't mean so much to me anymore. I've already broken her rules by forgiving her.

She likes me again . . for now . . until I do something wrong again. But it's like being grounded because she's always studying me . . watching everything I do so closely and waiting for me to do the wrong thing.

She's only my friend when no one else is around. She's only my friend when there's no chance to get too close to me.

She's careful around me now . . going to put her hand on mine but then pulling it away like my skin is poison. It's like we have to learn how to be best friends again . . she has to learn how to be comfortable around me . . I have to learn how to feel less when I'm around her. Benji says I shouldn't bother . . says I should forget about her but I told him I believe in second chances.

I know she's not going to change. I don't even know if I want her to change. I just know that I like to be near her. That when I'm near her I think that maybe one day I can catch up to her . . maybe one day I can walk the way she walks and let everyone look at me the way they look at her . . maybe one day I won't be scared anymore. I'll be strong like she is . . like Joan of Arc is too . . as long as I keep near them both maybe.

–*Gross! What are you doing with that?*– Jenna is seeing the book in front of me . . seeing the drawing I copied . . the dead bodies . . but she doesn't see how beautiful they are.

I quickly close my sketchbook. –*Nothing.*–

Jenna flips the book closed to read the cover . . –*Joan of Arc?*– she says . . rolling her eyes . . –*Isn't she like Rainbow Brite or something?*–

I tell her *no* . . tell her how Joan of Arc talked to ghosts . . how she fought in wars and everything. Jenna's face brightens . . remembering history class. *–Oh yeah yeah . . she's the one who went crazy. They had to burn her . . right?–*

I lower my head and Jenna acts like she let it slip out . . covers her mouth . . says *–sorry–* but she doesn't mean it. She knew what she was saying . . she knew she was talking about me . . about my dad going crazy and how I told her secrets about how I thought maybe I would go crazy too.

I try not to let it bother me.
I know she's only testing me.

She says things on purpose now to hurt me . . says them like they're accidents but I know they aren't. I think she does it so that we don't get too close . . so that we don't get as close as we did in my room that day. I think she's afraid of that . . of me . . of being too close to me. And I'd rather be friends like this because it's still better than not being friends at all . . and maybe . . slowly . . we can be friends like we were.

I'm too scared to be alone.

The pictures move across the screen but we can't hear what they're saying . . their voices are turned off and only their faces show that they even exist. Or maybe it's on so low that I just can't hear it . . I can only hear the noises outside . . a child yelling to his friends on a bicycle as they pass . . no cars going by . . the empty sound of Benji's neighborhood.

But I can hear him breathing against my throat.

The sun is still out . . peeking through the blinds in thin rectangles on the sofa . . little stripes of light on my skin like a zebra . . on the television too and it's like watching in on someone . . peeking through their blinds from the house across the street . . peeking into their perfect world to find things that aren't so perfect.

207

It's still early but I'm not worried about that. I don't have to rush home. I don't have to watch Malky . . not anymore . . now that Mom has quit her night job at the diner so she can be home with us . . with Malky. She should be home now . . or soon anyway. The diner was an hour away so she won't have that drive anymore.

I never knew why she drove so far when there are diners in our town and in the next town and in every town from here to the ocean. But I think I know now . . I think I know why she would change out of her uniform and let her hair down too before she got in the car . . I think I know just by looking around as Benji and I walked from the bus stop to his house . . the way the people all stare out their windows but look away whenever anyone catches them . . the way they leave their blinds down in the daytime . . their doors shut.

My mom didn't want anyone to know she worked in the diner. She didn't want anyone coming in who would say *–Oh Margaret I had no idea you worked here–* and pretend that it was nice to see her when really they would be thinking *–what a shame–* and whispering *–did you know–* to whoever it was they came in with.

Did you know about her husband?

Then when my mom would come back they would smile big lipstick smiles and tip her generously because of me and Malky and the pretty house that she wants to keep so bad despite its bad memories.

I'm glad she's not doing that anymore . . glad she quit even if it means that someday we might have to move into *Tricia Meadows* or somewhere else like it. I don't mind at all. I don't mind it when I'm here with Benji. And I can be here with him because she is home . . because Malky is sitting at the table with her drinking a glass of milk and smiling the way he only does at her because with me he smiles like a brother to his sister . . not the way he smiles for a mother. And she is . . she's trying to be our mom again.

That's more than I can say for Benji's mom.

When she's here she wishes he didn't exist . . that he would run away like a stray dog. —*Shoo*— she says to him when he comes near her and she swats his hand like he really is Dogboy. He doesn't say anything . . just covers his face with his hair and turns away from her and I get all sad inside like I want to wrap him up and take him with me just like a puppy that is hit and kicked by a mean person who doesn't want him.

–It's okay really. I don't see her much. She's never here– he tells me. I'm too scared of sounding like a stupid little girl to say anything except *–oh–* . . and besides . . I know what it's like to have people talk to you about your family . . to try to get you to open up about how much things hurt . . that it only hurts more when they do . . it feels better to keep it all inside where no one can know the way it twists you up in there. That's why I don't say anything . . that's why I let him tell me what he wants to tell me when he wants to. If I ask him it will only make him feel worse the way it feels when people ask me about my dad.

At least she's not here now . . it's not so bad then.

–You want something to drink?– . . lifting his head from my shoulder. I thought he was napping . . maybe he was . . maybe he's awake just now.

–Okay– I say and he gets up. I watch him walk through the tiny door frame and into the kitchen. I watch the way his hands move when he reaches into the cabinet and takes out two glasses to put them under the running water in the

sink . . his hands pale like the little patches of snow that stay around long after the rest of it has melted.

He sees me watching him . . catches me out of the corner of his eye and I can tell he gets embarrassed. His cheeks don't go red like mine . . but it doesn't take that to tell. I know I'm the only one in the world who gets to see him like this . . that he doesn't show this side of him outside . . that he's afraid to be this pretty and perfect to anyone but me because that is not the way he's supposed to be. He's supposed to be tougher than he is . . he's supposed to be angrier than he is . . and that's what he shows only he shows me the rest of him too.

I want to show him the rest of me. Now that his mother isn't home . . that we are alone in the empty house. We can do things that grown-ups do . . we can show ourselves to each other.

He isn't looking at me when he walks back into the room . . his eyes careful to watch the glasses in his hands . . watching so that the water doesn't spill onto the stained carpet.

He isn't watching the way my fingers tremble as I touch the bottom of my shirt . . lifting slowly. Only the silent faces

211

on the television are watching me . . only they can see the thin lines of sunlight on my stomach as I pull my sweater over my head and slip my arms out of the sleeves.

–Um . . – he stutters when he sees me . . when I put my hands behind my shoulder blades and pull the ends of my bra closer together so that I can pull them apart.

Benji stands there with the water in his hands . . his eyes open so wide like boys in the movies when girls in the movies do what I am doing. I can see myself in the glare on the television . . can see the way I bring my elbows into my sides to let the straps slide down over my arms.

I can feel my face turning red . . my heart beating so fast like a bird is trapped inside my chest and is struggling to get out . . the same way my body feels . . wanting to get out of my clothes and see my reflection naked on the television.

It's hard to open the button on my jeans with the way my hands are so nervous. I'm so scared and excited at the same time that my fingers are numb. The way his pants stick out where his thing is makes me nervous too . . knowing that I can do that to him . . and the button comes undone easily then and so does the next and the next and then I lean back with my jeans unbuttoned for him to see me.

I know he's scared too . . I know he doesn't know what to do and I don't know what to do either except for what I am doing . . sitting there . . because all I wanted to do was this.

I'm afraid to look in his eyes . . afraid it won't be him there . . that his eyes will be hungry instead . . will be sharp and cold the way I remember Avery's eyes when Jenna lay down for him on his sofa.

I keep my eyes on his stomach as he comes closer . . putting the glasses down on the coffee table and sitting down sideways on the sofa so that he can face me. I still don't look in his eyes when he touches my breast . . touches it softly like it will break if he touches too hard . . touching my face with his other hand and finally I look at him . . finally I let him look inside me and it's not at all like Avery . . it's like Benji only closer to me like there's no space between us.

I stand up . . letting his hands move along my sides like I'm slipping out of them . . letting my jeans catch on them and slide down as I'm standing up. I bite my lip to keep from screaming . . to keep control of everything I feel inside me when I feel his breath near where my body folds together.

Then I smile.

I know I'm as beautiful as the drawing of Joan of Arc in her transparent gown . . that to him I'm the most beautiful thing he has ever seen and that no matter what happens for the rest of our lives he will always remember me this way.

For this moment we are the only people in the world. For this moment I am pretty and everything is perfect.

But moments can be broken so quickly . . moments can be shattered the way the glass does when it falls . . fragments of it on the carpet . . tiny bits to remember of it.

Our moment is broken with the sound of a car pulling up to his house . . the sound of car doors opening . . closing . . muffled voices on the steps leading to the front door. It is like someone changed the channel on the television and we are trying to adjust to the new program that is on . . rushing to fasten the buttons . . to make my hands move faster than the ones at the front door and only able to pull my sweater in front of me when his mother walks in . . only enough time for Benji to stand between me and the door before her boyfriend steps into the kitchen.

–*What are you two doing here?*– she asks . . her voice like gasoline . . the smell of gasoline and the sting of it.

She has to hold on to the countertop to stand. She has to sway her head back and forth to be able to look straight at Benji. *He's* not looking at Benji though . . her boyfriend . . he's looking at me . . his mustache curled into a grin at the way I'm shivering under his glare . . the way my arms are folded over me with the sweater draped over them like a blanket that is too small to keep me warm.

–*Remember I live here*– Benji says to her. –*More than you do.*–

–*What's that supposed to mean?*– With every word I'm afraid she will fall down and hit her head on the corner of the table . . that she'll rest her head in a puddle of blood on the tile until we lift her neck back by her hair and wonder if she's still breathing.

–*You haven't been here in two days. That's what it means.*– He didn't tell me . . he never said. –*I wish next time you'd never come back!*– and I'm scared about how angry his voice is . . scared that something bad is going to happen.

–*Maybe I won't.*– She is laughing. Her boyfriend is holding on to her shoulder to help her stand steady. –*Or maybe I just won't let you back in next time you're out.*– And she keeps laughing like she heard somebody tell a joke but it doesn't fit somehow . . like the sound got switched with another show on the television.

Benji turns away from her . . his eyes pink around the edges . . his hands in tiny fists and his hair pushed behind his ears that are red with anger.

Her boyfriend opens his mouth for the first time . . he nods at me even though he's talking to her. *–Look at him trying to be a little man in front of his little lady over there.–* And that makes his mother laugh more . . makes her reach behind the toaster oven on the counter for a green-colored bottle with a cap that unscrews easily.

–Shut up.– But Benji doesn't say it like he wants to . . he only mumbles it and shakes his head. He shakes his head more when the boyfriend asks if he's going to introduce me to him . . when he asks me to come over and shake his hand because he knows when I do that he'll be able to see my breasts without the sweater over them.

–SHUT UP!– Benji shouts.

He ignores when the boyfriend keeps asking him *–what d'you say?–* over and over . . louder and louder. He ignores him when he lets go of his mother and stands with his hands in large fists . . his eyebrows curled up like a bull.

–*Come on Lacie. Let's get out of here.*– He stands in front of me so that I can pull my sweater on over my head as quickly as possible so that her boyfriend only gets to see me so fast that he won't even be able to tell what he's see-ing. Then I slip my feet into my sneakers . . I don't bother to tie them . . I can tie them outside . . I can tie them when we are away from here.

I grab my coat and wrap my bra up in it so that he can't see it . . so that he can't say anything and then I get up close to Benji and walk behind him to the door.

It's like his mother isn't there anymore . . she's sitting at the table with her mouth around the top of the bottle she found . . her eyes open but staring out somewhere that doesn't exist.

Her boyfriend is there though . . standing in front of the door and I've never been so scared of anyone in my whole life . . the way he is trying to scare Benji with his fists . . the way he is trying to stare at me with his eyes hungrier than I think Avery's could ever have been.

–Move . . *please*– Benji says and the man smiles at making Benji say please and I want to hold Benji so tight . . to run my hands through his hair the way I do for Malky when he climbs into my bed with nightmares. I want to tell him anything . . to do anything for him that will make him forget.

And when we get outside in the fresh air I just want to run. Pulling him by the hand and running in front of the wind. I want to run until I can't remember who I am . . run to our little house in the woods where the ground will keep us warm. I want to run until we are so tired that I forget that for a moment I saw in his eyes what I once saw in my dad's eyes . . until he can't remember that for a moment he thought maybe it would be better to be dead than alive.

day 77

Mandy lowers her voice when the girl walks by behind me . . the girl in our grade who wears her hair in pigtails and still wears buckled shoes and dresses that girls wear in 2nd grade. *–She's so retarded–* Mandy whispers . . rolls her eyes the way Jenna would if she were here. *–I heard she leaves the door open in the bathroom . . that's what Tina said . . that she sits there and everyone can see her. What's wrong with her?–*

–I know! What a freak.– Kara agrees with her . . but she would agree with her no matter what she said. If Mandy had said the girl was the prettiest girl in the world she would have said the same thing . . *–I know–* . . and leaning in closer as she said it . . exaggerating her expression . . because that's what you do when you fit in.

I don't say anything . . I don't even nod but they don't even notice.

I am so different from them now . . from Mandy with the way she flutters her eyes . . her eyes drowning in purple eye makeup . . her arms with goose bumps because it's too cold to be wearing a top that doesn't cover her belly button but she does anyway and I wonder if she even knows that she looks just as silly as the girl who walked by.

In September I would have nodded. I would have said *–I know–* the way Kara did and worry that I didn't really know . . worry that I might be wearing something that they would think was *retarded* and wonder if they talked about me putting my fingers in my mouth the way they do about that girl leaving the door open when she is in the girls' room.

I'm not that person anymore . . I'm different than I was in September when I wanted to be like them . . when I wanted to be liked . . when I wanted to pretend all the time the way they do . . the way they pretend not to have their own opinions or feelings and not to care and that nothing is wrong ever.

They complain about their parents and not getting enough money to buy things they don't need. They complain about having to do homework and take tests and not being able to spend more time sitting here making fun of anyone that doesn't look exactly the way they think they should. That's what makes them happy . . and I don't know what about it ever made me think I wanted to be that way.

It used to be different when Jenna wasn't around . . Mandy and Kara would be different. They would stop pretending a little bit. But that was before high school . . before they realized they didn't need Jenna . . that nobody else in the other grades thought Jenna was such a big deal the way kids in our grade do.

I guess that's why they talk about her now . . why they're not afraid to talk about her the way they do about everyone else. Kara pushes her hair away from her face . . tightens her lips and squints the way Jenna does when she's annoyed and they both laugh. They both start to mimic all the little things Jenna does . . the things they've tried so hard to copy.

–Lacie what's wrong with you . . she's meanest to you– Mandy asks when I don't join them.

I shrug my shoulders. I don't know. I wasn't going to do that . . to make fun of her. I would just stop being friends with her first.

–I don't know why Avery is still going out with her– Kara says. *–He's sooo perfect.–* . . And I want to say that she used to think Jenna was perfect too.

–She told me she didn't even do it with him yet!– Mandy tells us . . spilling out Jenna's secrets and spreading them around because neither of them care. *–I know he's done it before . . Nicole told me. She said he's going to dump her soon if she doesn't.–*

They laugh and I want to find Jenna and tell her . . to tell her she doesn't have to do anything she doesn't want because the thought of her doing that for him makes me sick because he is supposed to love her.

–I would do it with him– Kara says and I know it's a lie . . I know she would never do it with anyone . . I know she is just as afraid as the rest of us because she told me once when she was at my house. That's why she looks at me when she says it . . begging me not to tell her secret the way Mandy is telling Jenna's.

–I would too– Mandy says because they both want to be better than Jenna in some way . . they both want to leave her behind the way she has left me behind. And I know the rest of high school is a race for them . . to be the first to do

everything . . and I know I don't want to be in it. I know I want things to happen when they are supposed to happen . . not when they think they should.

–*What about you?*– Mandy now turning to me. –*Have you done it with Benji?*– rubbing her hands together like a fly . . wanting to know everything . . wanting to wrap up everything I tell her to spread it around to anyone who will listen.

I can't look at her . . I can't look at Kara either because she is the same way if only a little less obvious about it.

I think about Benji . . about his hands on my hips . . about the only time he saw me naked and how it was nothing like what they are talking about. I put my fingers to my mouth . . not wanting to speak . . not to them.

I shake my head.

–*I didn't think so.*– Mandy says it like it is a dare I didn't finish . . like there is something wrong with me for not doing it.

That's when they start talking about him . . saying things like I'm not even here . . like he doesn't exist to me the way he does. –He's weird anyway– Mandy says and I give her a look but it doesn't stop her. –I heard they call him Dogboy because he's the one killing all those cats.–

–That's not true!– I know I shouldn't say anything . . that I'm only playing into them . . but I can't help myself . . I can't stop from being angry and that only makes them try harder to upset me because they know it's working.

–I heard they call him that because he likes dogs– Kara says. –But I guess that's why he likes you.– They both cover their mouths and start laughing as hard as they can.

I know she's only teasing . . that I'm supposed to laugh too . . that saying things you don't mean is part of pretending. But I can't. I can only think of him in my bedroom . . waiting for it to get dark . . for my mother to call me down for dinner and knowing he has to go home to where he never wants to be. They don't know anything about him. I won't listen to them making fun of him.

I don't say anything. I pick up my backpack and push my chair away from the table. I won't even look at them as I start to walk away . . walk through the tiny rows of chairs filled with talking voices where it's easy to get lost.

–*LACIE* . . – I hear Kara shout. –*We were only joking!*– but I don't turn back. In September I would have come back . . I would have let them tease me more . . but it's not even me . . it's him. I won't let them make fun of him.

–*Who needs her anyway?*– Mandy says and it is the last thing I hear before I get too far into the crowded faces.

*   *   *

–*Who are they . . those girls?*– her hands folded on the table in front of her . . throwing her head back to where I can see Mandy and Kara talking . . looking over here every once in a while and laughing when they see that I'm look-ing at them.

–*They used to be my friends*– I say and Gretchen closes her eyes then opens them again . . slowly . . letting me know she knows exactly what I mean when I say *used to*.

I don't know what it is about her . . what makes me able

to say anything to her . . what makes me want to say everything to her. Maybe it's the way her eyes are the same color as I remember Jenna's were the first time I saw her . . maybe that's just the way anyone's eyes look when you need somebody to talk to so bad that you feel the muscles pull on the back of your throat.

–Why aren't they your friends anymore?–

I look down at my own hands . . squeezing them together so tight it scares me. I let go. *–They think I'm weird–* I say and pull my hands under the table . . putting them under my thighs to keep them from doing anything that might make Gretchen think I'm weird too.

–It's better to be weird than fake– she says.

I look up at her . . she is smiling at me. It's like she knows everything about me . . about them. I want to ask her how she can have everything so figured out . . how she can never let anything bother her.

–It's easier to be fake though– I say . . covering my face with my hair and looking down at my hands again.

She smiles wider then. *–You remind me of someone–* she

tells me . . tells me I sound the same . . the same black hair but mine's more curly. *–She would say the same thing.–* . . I smile a little bit but I don't know if it's a good thing or a bad thing . . but she seems happy that I remind her so I guess it's a good thing and I smile too.

–How come you don't have any friends?– I ask and suddenly she looks sad and I wish that I hadn't said anything.

It's her turn to let her hair fall in front of her face . . long hair . . wavy and blond like models in the old magazines that Jenna's dad keeps locked away from her little brother because the models sometimes don't have any clothes on.

–I haven't wanted any friends . . not for a while anyway.–

I wonder if that means that she does now . . or if it means she doesn't want me for a friend either. *–Why not?–* I ask.

–Because– . . she takes a breath . . looking for words I think . . *–I usually lose people.–* And I can see that maybe she doesn't have everything figured out the way I thought . . that maybe she's not as strong as she acts . . at least not for a second before she smiles again . . says *–nevermind–* . . that it was a long time ago in another place.

It's not much . . I touch her hand . . only for a second . . but it's enough to let her know that I've lost people too. Behind her eyes I can see so many places and things she's seen that I know I never have . . I don't see what they are . . just that they're there and that they are different from all the rumors everyone has said about her.

I ask her about those places . . about where she came from before she came here this year . . about where she was for three years before coming back.

She says she doesn't want to talk about it . . that some-day maybe she'll tell me . . *–Maybe tomorrow–* she says and I smile because she doesn't have to if she doesn't want to. Besides I can wait . . I don't need to know everything all at once.

–Let's talk about something else– she says.

She asks me about my drawings . . about the one of the three dead bodies in the field . . asks if I've finished and I reach into my bag and take out my sketchbook . . flip through pages to get to it.

–Wait . . wait– putting her hand between the pages *–I want to see them all–* she says and turns back to the first page.

She looks at every picture . . looks at them carefully. I put my fingers in my mouth . . nervous she won't like them . . nervous that she'll want to lose me too after this . . nervous because she spends too much time on the first picture . . nervous because no one has ever seen most of them . . because they are like tiny secrets caught on a page . . nervous because I like her. I want to be friends with her.

She stops looking at the pages . . looks at me and I cross my fingers inside my mouth . . biting down on them . . waiting for her to say something mean the way Jenna would.

–*These are beautiful.*– Then she smiles at me . . smiles the way you do to your very best friend and flips to the next picture.

day 81

I rub my finger over the porcelain rooftops . . around the window frames . . wishing I could take one of these little houses and make it real for me and him to live in. Or maybe if we could make ourselves small enough to fit into these we could live in my room forever . . safe where no one could find us.

Benji says he likes that . . says it's a pretty idea the way he always says when I tell him something I'm dreaming of. But that's all it is . . a pretty idea.

In my bedroom we can have pretty ideas and dreams. I can climb onto the bed next to him. We can lie on my bed together side by side . . our clothes on and under the covers . . staring up at the ceiling painted all white like a sky covered over with clouds . . the walls like a castle with blue flowers painted on pink wallpaper. We can pretend the walls are strong and made of bricks instead of thin plaster . . are strong enough to keep our problems out.

Outside the light is going dark and I have to feel around to find his hand . . hold it against my stomach and in here everything is perfect. There is nothing but what we want there to be . . and the ghosts can come watch us . . moving behind the walls and into my room . . and they are like all the people in our kingdom and we are their prince and princess. We can lie here forever and be looked at by them . . safe and together.

But none of it's real.
The walls are too thin.
Too many things scratch away at our dreams.

Outside my window where the cars drive slowly over the icy streets . . where dead trees sway in the wind like the skeletons of ghosts . . out there our dreams disappear. Because when we step outside my room we go back to being ourselves. I go back to being Lacie . . he goes back to being Dogboy . . and my room is no longer the castle in the snow like I pretend . . it goes back to being another cold room in a house where we can't afford to turn up the heat too high.

I roll over . . resting my elbow on the bed and holding my chin with my hand.

–*When is he moving in?*– I ask . . hoping he says months . . or weeks even . . just not days . . not today or tomorrow. I don't want to think about Benji having to live with that man . . his mother's boyfriend with the curly mustache and angry eyes.

–*I'm not sure*– he says quietly.

I ask how long he'll stay.

–*Not long probably. They never stay too long.*–

I wish he could live here . . move in with me so he didn't have to live with his mother or her boyfriend. I wish he could stay in here and I'd even make a place on the floor for him if my mom wanted it that way. Even if he stayed in Malky's room . . or in the living room. But my mom would never . . she's barely getting used to him coming over at all . . and she's still not so sure about us being in my room with the door closed but she says she's trying to trust me.

Maybe we could live in the woods. We could bring sleeping bags into the broken house and make it our own. I would bring things from my house . . things to eat and wear and I would draw pictures to tape onto the walls so it would feel like a home.

–It'll be okay– he says . . but I think he is trying to convince himself more than me . . says this isn't the first time and he was fine all those times before. I don't believe him though . . it's different this time. I can tell it's different by the way his voice shakes.

He puts his hand through my hair and I don't know why but all I feel is afraid.

I can hear Malky on the stairs . . racing up them two at a time and I know that we don't have time to say another word about this to each other . . that Malky is coming to knock on my door and tell me to come down to eat. Benji will have to go then because my mother is trying to make us a family again with family dinners. He'll have to go and I will have to keep my fingers crossed under the table and hope for him to be okay.

–LACIE! DINNER!– my brother shouts . . his small hands start banging on my door.

–I guess I should go– Benji says and I tell him he can

stay if he wants . . he can wait in here for me to finish. He doesn't want to though . . says he doesn't want to screw up my family just because his is. I want to tell him that he can't screw up my family any worse by staying but I keep my mouth closed instead.

–LACIE!– Malky yells again and I tell him I'm coming.

I straighten out my clothes in the mirror . . smooth out the wrinkles and use my fingers like a comb to fix my hair. When I open the door Malky is there trying to push his face into my room. –Were you kissing?– he laughs and I put my hand over his face and push him away from the door and he runs away again down the stairs.

Benji follows me down and I keep wanting to turn around . . to look at him for a little bit longer because maybe then it won't seem like he's gone when he goes.

My mom is watching from the kitchen . . standing with a kitchen towel in her hand . . her hair pulled back like the way she wore it when she worked at the diner. She's waiting there for him to leave . . watching so he doesn't kiss me.

I stand behind him as he opens the door and the cold air races in . . I want to hold on to him but I know my mother will yell if we leave the door open . . so I keep still. I wave and he says *—bye—* and when he closes the door behind him I can't help feeling afraid that I will never see him again . . that I've lost him.

—Is everything okay?— my mother asks from the kitchen.

I wipe my eyes and turn away from the door. *—Yeah. It's fine—* I tell her.

—Then it's time to eat— she says and I say *—okay—* . . wipe my nose with my sleeve and walk slowly into the dining room with its bright lights and warm food.

day 85

He was supposed to come over today.

My mother is at Malky's basketball game. I didn't go because he is supposed to be here with me . . he is supposed to be watching the faces move across the television . . our eyes staring at the same things.

He never even called.

Only the ghosts are here to keep me from being alone . . watching the television even though it isn't on.

day 87

He didn't come to school today.

He didn't come to school yesterday.

I haven't heard his voice in three days and I think I'm going to die.

I called from the pay phone at school . . dialed his number and had to hang up twice because each time I didn't know what I would say if he answered.

The third time I didn't hang up and his mother answered. I told her it was me . . –*Lacie*– . . and she said –*who who?*– and I said I was the girl with the black curly hair and asked her if I could speak to Benji please.

–He's not here– she said and I asked where he was . . it was none of my business she said . . asked if I was the one making their phone ring off the hook all morning . . if I was the girl who woke her up and I shook my head hoping she would see me through the telephone . . hoping she would believe me. *–It was better when this thing was shut off!–* she yelled and then hung up the phone.

I held my end to my ear until I heard the dial tone . . until the dial tone turned into the electronic operator's voice saying if I liked to make a call I should please hang up and try again.

The rest of the day at school is like sleepwalking. Passing through halls from one class to the next and nothing seeming to happen in between. The colors of the lockers changing from one hall to the next . . orange into green into yellow and I only find where I'm going by moving the same way I do every day.

Now I watch the clock on the wall and wait . . watch the long red hand spin around so fast the way animals spin around a circus ring . . but no matter how fast the seconds go the two smaller hands never seem to move and I think maybe time is broken . . or only the seconds work and I'll never get forward . . I'll never make it to the end of last period and into the cold air where maybe I won't feel so trapped by the things I think.

–*Lacie are you with us?*– It's Mrs. Carlyle's voice . . my teacher's voice. I can hear her . . only it's like hearing through a wall . . like the way the ghosts must hear my voice at night when I make quiet noises while they watch through holes in the wallpaper.

I'm not sure if I ever try to say anything . . I'm not sure if I can turn away from facing the window where the sky goes on forever . . I keep trying to find where it meets the ground but I can't . . the snow matching the color of the sky or the other way around . . I can't be sure . . either way it's impossible to tell the difference and I wonder if I could run to where they touch and if I would disappear when I got there.

–*Perhaps we should get you a pacifier . . maybe a blanket too and you could go in the back and take a nap!*– It's her voice again . . only closer . . the smell of her perfume hanging over my desk . . the low roar of the other kids laughing . . it all breaks through at once and makes me deaf.

–Hmmm?– looking up at her . . her eyebrows like two fat caterpillars over her eyes . . her suit with a stale scent like

an old basement but covered up with perfume so I feel sick
to my stomach.

*–Take your fingers OUT of your mouth . . turn . .
around . . and PAY attention.–* Each word pronounced like
the clear sound of a bell. *–This isn't a nursery school.–*

I do as she says . . I do it automatically . . take my fingers
away from my face and wipe them on my jeans . . pull my
knees forward and let my eyes rest on the letters she has
scribbled on the blackboard.

–Now let's see if we can stay focused– Mrs. Carlyle says to
the class as she walks back toward the front of the room . .
begins talking about the paragraphs in our textbook as the
whispers start up behind me . . their words like tiny flames
at the back of my neck . . their eyes on me . . making my
face go red.

I need him.
I need him with me here right now.

I look up at the clock again . . twenty minutes left and I
hope I can keep from crying until then.

I can't go to his house. I can't ask Avery for a ride again . . Jenna would never let him. She barely talks to me at all as it is. She's even stopped talking to me when no one else is around . . mostly she doesn't even look at me when she passes . . not since I started being friends with Gretchen . . when I stayed being friends with her even after Jenna told me not to.

She won't talk to me now.
I was only good to her when I did what she told me to do.

I could walk to his house . . I have the way memorized . . the number of steps from the school to his front door. I could find it on my own but that doesn't matter. His mother said he wasn't there anyway. Maybe he's home now . . but if he's not then I will have to talk to her . . or worse I'll have to talk to Roy her boyfriend.

It's better to go to our place in the woods . . our secret place. And if I hope hard enough . . if I keep my fingers crossed tight enough inside my coat pockets . . then maybe he will hear me . . maybe he will be there waiting for me too. If he knows how much I need him he will be.

It's tough to find the way in the winter . . the snow fallen over the path and the branches crossing in front of my eyes . . but there's enough space between the trees to know which way to go.

There are no footprints though.
But maybe he took another way.

The snow crunches underneath my steps the way Christmas lights do when you walk on them accidentally . . the sound echoing in the empty woods . . bouncing back at me to let me know how alone I am in here.

I can feel the ghosts above me . . floating through the branches like smoke that is so clear like the water that drips into my hair from the melting snow above me. I can't see them or hear them but I feel them . . the way they look . . the music they make gliding through the wind. I'm afraid of them . . I'm afraid of them getting too close to me the way they got too close to my dad . . afraid they want to take me to the place where he is . . afraid they will if I don't have someone to hold on to.

Only the tops of the crumbling walls poke out above the ground . . through the snow . . gray cinder blocks like a castle standing in the clouds. I know he's not here . . know it deep inside me but also deep inside me I can't give up hoping . . hoping that with the next step I'll see the messy strands of his hair . . so bright like the yellow of the sun and then everything I'm afraid of will melt the way the snow on the tree limbs is melting and straightening out the curls that hang in front of my face.

But every step closer I take only makes the ghosts circle faster . . only makes them howl like angry birds circling . . and they seem less like angels now and more like the giants in Malky's nightmares.

The house seems less like the castle in my drawings now and more like the prison cell where they kept Joan of Arc before they killed her.

I climb down into it anyway . . maybe he will feel closer in there . . surrounded by the walls he has leaned against.

How long should I wait?
How long should I stay here in the cold?

Probably not at all. Probably I should climb into my bed

and pull the covers over my face and hide from the world until he comes to find me.

Maybe I should stay for a little while. It feels good to be cold . . feels like something besides being numb . . something besides the ache inside.

I lie down in the snow . . letting it hold me the way water holds you when you put your arms out and lean back. I write our names in the snow . . *Lacie* . . *Benji* . . write our birthdays . . write our eye color and hair color . . our phone numbers . . our addresses . . because if I write everything into the earth then maybe it will stay there . . maybe it will become permanent like the soil . . maybe by writing it I will change everything.

I stop when I can't think of anything left to write down . . when the floor is covered with letters and numbers scratched into the snow . . with my footprints going back and forth between all the things I've written so it's like I'm part of the words and that somehow gives them more meaning.

There's nothing left to do but wait . . to lie down in the snow with my arms spread out to my sides. I begin to move them up and down . . back and forth . . my legs side to side.

It must be beautiful from above . . a perfect snow angel for the ghosts to see.

I close my eyes . . think of how beautiful it would be if someone came to find me . . if I froze in the snow with angel wings pressed into the ground . . my lips a pretty purple-blue . . my eyelids pink and my skin pale . . how beautiful they would say I was . . how perfect.

day 89

Jenna stops in front of me . . she holds out her hand. I didn't think she was going to stop . . the way she walked down the hall with her neck stiff . . her eyes straight ahead to not look at me on purpose . . to not look where she knows I will be . . in front of the classroom that I have to be inside of when the bell rings.

She knows I am here . . that I'm here every day waiting for her . . even the last week when I knew she would not talk to me. The first few days she made excuses . . –*Lacie I can't stop to talk. I'm late.*– . . the next day I only got –*hi*– and after that only a wave. Yesterday and the day before I didn't even get that.

That's the way it works when you are not friends anymore. It's not a big fight or a very secret secret . . it happens little by little after that. It happens in shorter talks and waves in the hall until they don't stop to talk anymore and you are standing in front of your classroom knowing no one is coming to stand with you. Because that is what happens in high school . . those are the rules and you don't have to follow them to make them apply to you.

Every day that passes without her talking to me will erase me that much more . . take away one memory at a time until there is nothing left and she can walk by me and make herself believe that we were never friends. I wonder which parts of me she has chosen to forget already . . which she is holding on to to be the last.

Maybe she can pretend so easily but I can't.
Nothing will make me forget we were best friends.

And for a quick second I think maybe she has changed her mind . . that she is going to give me another chance . . standing there in front of me . . her eyes the way I remember.

She's holding out her hand. I open my mouth to say I'm sorry . . sorry for everything . . sorry that I'm so strange and that I will be different . . anything . . as long as she is standing there I can take everything back that has happened between us and we can be like we were.

Before I can speak she interrupts me. *–Here. This is for you–* she says and I look down to see she is holding a folded piece of paper in her hand.

I stare at it.
It's a note.

I knew it was stupid to wish. I know wishes don't come true . . I know that after she walks away from me today we will become strangers. One of her new friends will point to me and ask her *–Aren't you friends with her?–* and I'll hear Jenna say *–God! That was like 4th grade–* and she'll say it like it was a flu she had.

–Well take it!– she says . . but I'm afraid. I'm afraid it's a note telling me everything she doesn't like about me.

Then I see it's from him . . his handwriting . . the letters of my name the way he writes them . . not curly the way Jenna does. That only makes me more afraid.

I've made up my mind that he ran away . . that he walked out to the highway and walked alongside the cars at night . . just far enough from the side of the road so the headlights couldn't catch him the way Gretchen told me she had done two years ago.

I'm scared that his note will tell me it's true so I don't want to read it . . as long as I don't read it I can still hope . . can still keep my fingers crossed and lie in my bed at night and think that maybe I will see him tomorrow . . maybe. I won't have to think about him living in the streets of some city where no one cares if you have a name . . where no one cares that when he hides his face behind his hair it means he's shy or nervous . . that when he says things like *never-mind* and *it's okay* he really means nothing is okay that he needs me to hold him close.

Jenna starts shaking her hand at me . . the folded piece of paper making a cracking noise like a kite trying to stand still in a strong wind.

I take it . . placing it carefully between my fingers.

—Did you see him? Did he give this to you?— I ask her. I want to know where . . I want to know what he said . . what he was wearing . . the way he stood and the way his voice sounded.

Jenna rolls her eyes and folds her arms in front her. *—No—* she says. *—He gave it to Avery. Avery went to pick him up for school and he gave him this.—* She says it the way I've seen her talk when she has to answer questions from her mom . . like having to give the note to me is a chore . . like I'm just something that annoys her now and the quicker I'm done with the better.

–*Thanks*– I say but I can't look at her anymore . . I look at my name written on the paper. She doesn't say anything . . just walks away and I'm afraid that when I unfold the page I will be losing the two most important people to me in the same seconds.

The kids in the hall begin to hurry into the rooms as the bell rings . . disappearing behind holes . . running to hide . . but I stay in the hallway . . open the note . . take short quick breaths before I read.

> *Lacie*–
> *Meet me after school. At the cornfield.*

I read it ten times . . eight words . . ten times because it doesn't mean anything the first nine. The tenth time it does . . it means he's not gone . . that I will see him . . one hour from now at the spot of our first kiss. Nothing else matters . . because I'm going to see him . . nothing after that matters.

I put the letter to my lips . . fold it up and shove it in my pocket so it's close to me . . so when I think I can't breathe anymore I can touch it and know it's okay.

–*You're late*– my teacher says when I walk in.

–*I'm sorry*– I whisper and he says to take a seat.

* * *

On purpose I won't look ahead of me . . I won't look to the place where the dead grass turns into dirt covered with the scratched lines from the plow . . lines frozen and cut into the ground like the pictures of dry planets in textbooks.

I look down at my sneakers . . my stomach so nervous inside that I have to concentrate not to fall down.

I look side to side at the kids standing beside trees or huddled on the ground by the school walls . . their heads just under the windows so that they can smoke cigarettes without anyone seeing them from inside.

I look up at the sky where the clouds have all gone away and the blue is so bright that it hurts my eyes and I think how strange it is to have a bright day in winter . . how in winter the sky only looks right if it's gray.

But I won't look straight ahead . . I don't want to see him standing so far away . . alone . . like a scarecrow on a dead field with nothing to scare away.

Or worse . . if he's not there at all.

The buses are pulling away from the school . . fifteen or more of them. The engines roar to life . . rumbling down across the open fields like an army . . charging over the hills and only the few trees and the crisscrossing power lines to keep them from blocking out everything. The noise coming down upon me and I feel so small . . feel so weak and I know I can never be like Joan of Arc . . I could never be brave like her and I can feel myself collapsing inside.

–Lacie . . Lacie.–

I can hear my name . . spoken in static . . the signal lost in the roar of the buses and fractured into pieces of my name so that I have to wait to be sure of what I heard.

–Lacie?–

I look up then.

I see Benji standing against the sky with the sun behind him.

My feet are in the exact spot where he kissed me sixty-one days ago. I can still feel the way his lips felt against mine . . can still remember the sour taste of his mouth . . the way his fingers felt on the small of my neck. I put my fingers to my mouth to remember better the way it felt . . the way I felt when he came toward me.

It's not the same today . . the way he walks is slower . . heavier. It's colder too today. His worn coat with the tear on the right shoulder where the stuffing pokes out the way it does on my stuffed raccoon that I got when I was 5 years old . . the raccoon that sits in the corner of my bedroom where I shoved all my stuffed animals months ago before Jenna came over one day . . and the stuffing in his coat makes me sad the same way having my raccoon in the corner does. It's the kind of sad that comes when you know there is something you can do to change it but know you won't and don't know for sure why.

It's not until he steps next to me so close the toes of

our shoes touch that I see the bruise around his eye . . the skin soft and purple and so sore that I'm afraid to touch it because I know it will make him squint and pull his head away.

I don't have to use words to ask him.
He doesn't have to use them to answer either.

I don't wait for him the way I always do . . I lean into him . . take him by the back of his neck and kiss him. I want to swallow him . . to keep him inside me and keep him safe the way pregnant women keep their babies safe. I want every little bit of him inside me.

And I think I'm beginning to understand Jenna and Avery . . the look in their eyes when they touch each other. I think I understand how their eyes grow wider . . hungry . . how they each want to pull the other one so close that they become siamese.

Only it's different.

They are hungry for the way it feels on the outside against their skin. I am hungry for the feelings inside that are so deep under my skin that I can feel them inside against my bones.

–I love you.–

The words are my words. The words are coming from my mouth . . slipping from my tongue and sliding under my front teeth. They feel like strangers in my mouth. I don't remember the last time I said them . . not even to my mother . . always saying *–you too–* when she would say them to me . . not since the last person I said them to left me forever.

–I love you.– . . but my words get lost on the cold breeze that turns our skin pink and our lips to ice.

He doesn't say them back.
All that is warm in him is gone . . frozen.

I don't need him to say anything to know he is going to leave me forever too . . I don't have to wait for the words when he starts speaking to know what they will mean.

–I'm moving Lacie. I'm going to live with my dad in Portland.– He puts his head against my shoulder but I don't feel it. I don't feel anything. I feel myself falling apart and there are pieces of me all over the ground . . a million

pieces like leaves blown off the branches and I'm only a ghost now like the trees are in winter.

–I can't live with her anymore.– He's trying to explain . . trying to say it in a way that will make sense . . but it will never make sense . . no matter how he says it . . it won't stop hurting.

He tries to hold me steady.
He tries to keep me from shaking.

–I spoke to my dad yesterday . . he said I should come.– Portland? It doesn't sound like a real place after I say it over and over again so many times in my head. It's too far away to mean anything . . it's too far away to understand.

I should have let him live in my bedroom. I could have hidden him under blankets when my mom or Malky were around . . I could have brought food up to him the way kids do on television when they hide pets in their room.

I should never have loved him . . I should never love anyone because it ends up being worse than being alone.

–Lacie? Say something please– . . putting his hand over mine . . closing my fingers so tight in his but I don't feel them.

What does he want me to say?
How does he want me to say it when I can't even breathe?

Nothing is worth saying anyway . . not when nothing matters . . not when there is no reason to hope anymore . . no reason to keep my fingers crossed or to repeat things in my head to try to make them come true because none of it ever will.

Maybe Jenna was right . . maybe I was just being a baby all those times I dreamed of things like castles in the clouds . . all those pictures I draw . . the girl who looks like me in her ripped gown. Maybe none of it means anything because that's how it feels standing here . . feeling nothing . . feeling empty . . a fire in my stomach but nothing to burn once my bones have melted.

Maybe our broken house in the woods is only that . . broken.

Broken like all the promises that he said in his voice but

I know now it was only the ghosts talking . . lying to me . . lying the way the giants do in Malky's dreams when they tell him it won't hurt when they sew his eyes closed.

Broken like I am inside . . where I've always been broken and it has nothing to do with my dad or with Jenna or with Benji because it's my fault for caring too hard . . it's my fault for not being like everyone else . . and I'm never going to be fixed because it's not something that can be fixed by hoping.

I pull away from him . . pull away like he is poison.
–*I love you*– he says.

It's too late . . everything is too late.
I back away . . he doesn't move.

No. It's too late for everything now. Too late to stand here watching his eyes change color as the sun moves in and out behind the clouds that have come from nowhere . . the clouds that carry the ghosts on them . . the ghosts coming to laugh at me . . to let me know they tricked me . . that I can never be happy but they let me think I could for a little while only so it will hurt that much more.

If I'm never going to see him again I want it to start now. Not in one hour . . not in one day . . because that will only make those hours worse than any others . . knowing he won't be with me once the hands on the clock move.

I turn away from him . . walk at first . . things far away getting closer and I know that I'm running then . . running so fast but I can't feel my legs . . can't feel my arms swinging as I run . . can't feel the wind sting as it blows over the tears frozen to my eyelashes . . can't feel anything except the fire on the inside of my chest that feels like a sun bursting and exploding a thousand times at once.

–Lacie! Wait!–

And I have to run until I can't hear him shout anymore . . until his voice fades into static and then into nothing so if I looked back I would only see his lips move the way they do in very old movies without any talking.

I have to run until I can't remember the way he looks or the sound of his voice. I have to run so far that my memories can't find me.

I never belonged here . . I never belonged anywhere and now I'm going to make it right . . I'm going to hide away forever. If I can make it there . . if I can run that fast . . I will.

The streets are empty . . the driveways are empty. There is only me . . running through the middle of the street with trees evenly spaced on both sides of me . . houses on either side placed in neat rows like they were dropped from the sky to make a map that is perfect to look at from above.

I don't know how long I've been running.
Maybe one hour . . more?

It's all like a dream . . like the set of a movie that has no other characters . . only me. And maybe the world is as pretty and perfect as it seems on the outside . . maybe it is and there are things that don't fit in it like the cats being killed . . like me . . and maybe those things need to be erased like mistakes in a drawing.

I see the sun through my tears . . it sparkles in them and everything twinkles like the first few flakes of a snowstorm and something about that makes me stop running . . something about being able to see something so beautiful in the middle of so much that's painful.

Maybe that's how it is when you give up.
Maybe you can't see beautiful things until then . . and when you do they are too beautiful to hold on to.

Maybe that's what my dad saw.
Maybe he was right.

I nearly fall down when the car honks its horn twice behind me . . so close that if I collapse its tires will run me into the pavement.

The car slows.
I step aside and it misses me.

I can feel the ground under my sneakers for the first time . . the cold on my face for the first time and my fingers so numb they burn like ice water under the frozen surface of a pond. And everything so numb inside and slowly that starts to go away too and I can feel my stomach again like someone has a hand in me tugging on it to pull it out.

The brakes screech on the car and the tires slide on the ice . . it moves in slow motion away from me.

I step over to the sidewalk . . falling to my knees and covering my mouth because I think I'm going to throw up but I'm dry inside and nothing comes out.

I worry that when I open my eyes the beauty I saw will be gone . . that I will feel the way I did two minutes ago when I wanted nothing but to run . . to run to my house where the stairs would move as I ran up them . . swaying and I would try hard to keep from passing out. And when I got to my room I would have thrown off my clothes . . I would have seen myself in the mirror and only seen something that needed to be erased . . something that needed to be lost and I would have gone into the bathroom where I could erase myself down the drain.

The sun saved me.
I'm afraid when I open my eyes I won't see it anymore.
I'm afraid that maybe I've gone crazy.

When I open my eyes again the world is blue. A safe shade of blue . . a perfect shade. Nothing anyone does . . nothing anyone says can make that go away . . can make the sky dangerous or ugly and I know that I need to be like the sky . . I need to stay . . I need to remember . . I need to let the sun warm me and learn to let the darkness pass when it's time.

I need to stop running.
I need to sit still for a moment and breathe.

I lie down in the grass with my feet on the curb . . my heart pounding so fast that I feel it in my wrists and in my neck. I can hear the car door open . . the person coming over to me . . can hear him whispering and swearing . . worried that he didn't miss me when he thought he did . . that maybe it took a second for me to realize it and to fall down to the side of the road.

That's when I think maybe I'm already dead . . maybe the car did hit me and this is what it feels like when the ghosts take you . . only I don't hear them . . I don't hear the ghosts laughing . . I don't hear them circling over me the way I do when they hurt me.

And that is when I know . . that is when I understand that it's better to feel the ache inside me like demons scratching at my heart than it is to feel numb the way a dead body feels when you touch it. It's better to wait for the beautiful things . . to stare at them for as long as they last . . to hold on as tight as you can before they disappear. And it might hurt so bad inside . . but it's better to wait for the next beautiful thing than to never look for any again.

–Girl? Hello? You alright?–

The man's words are like his hand poking me . . waking me and I smile.

I smile because the sky is so blue . . because it sparkles through the tears that I can taste on my fingers. I smile because as long as I can breathe I can hope and if I can hope then maybe I can learn to live in a perfect world where I don't belong.

The man doesn't care about hoping or about the color of the sky though. He only hopes I'm not dead . . and when he knows I'm not he asks if I need a ride somewhere . . that walking in the middle of the street is only good for getting killed.

I know.
I know and that is why I was walking there.

–That's okay. I don't need a ride– I tell him after he helps me stand up.

I'm not going home . . I don't want him to drive me. He is worried . . he thinks for sure he hit me and that I'm delirious . . that I must have hit my head pretty hard against the curb when he was trying to keep his car from spinning on the ice.

He asks me again if I'm okay . . asks as he is already moving toward his car whose engine is screaming to go . . asks with breath like gasoline . . and I tell him I'm fine and he says *–if you say so–* and the back wheels spin on the ice as he disappears around the next turn.

I'm okay because I know I haven't lost him yet.
I know it is not too late.

It takes a second to think . . to see the houses look the same on every street . . but then I pick out the little things . . the swing set in the backyard of one house . . the broken window with the plastic taped over it at another house . . and I know I am not far . . I only have to go a little farther before the houses end and the trees start to grow thicker except where there is a path worn into the dirt where I know he will be this time.

I walk quickly . . the branches scraping my skin as I brush against them . . not caring if they leave little red scars on my hands . . not caring about anything but seeing Benji sitting on the dirt floor in the house where I wrote our names.

I walk as quick as I can because even if I can't see him tomorrow or the next day or the next year even I know I can see him today. I know I can still say all the things I want to say to him and as long as we know each other's secrets then we are never far away from each other.

He's there.
I know he's there before I even get close enough.

I know even before I see the wind blowing his hair over the half-built wall. I know before he stands up to face the sound of my footsteps . . before I see him smile and show me his eyes so safe and blue the way the sky looks . . before I see the bruise on his face that makes me cry and makes me remember that it is not about me that he is going to go away . . that the problems in the world are not mine alone and that I don't have to be so afraid to face them because there will always be someone near to face them with me.

–*Lacie.*– The way he says my name is filled with everything I feel and I let him hold me as I hold him and we keep each other from falling down too fast.

–*I hoped you would come*– he says. He shows me his hand . . his fingers crossed the way he has seen me do a million times. –*I love you Lacie Johnson.*–

I smile. I smile because he really does. He loves the strange little things I do . . the way I say the wrong things sometimes . . the way my face turns red when I smile. He loves everything about me and that is not going to change just because he is in Portland and I am here. He loves me and that means even if I am different from everyone else there is still someone out there who wishes everyone was exactly like me.

I take his hand . . move my legs beneath him . . pull him so he is holding himself over me . . and I rest on his arms with my hair on the ground.

I close my eyes as he traces the shape of my bones by running his fingers over my face . . along my cheeks and across my lips. And this is what my dad never understood . . these are feelings that make up for everything that hurts . . like you are going to disappear inside somebody else but it's okay because that somebody else is somebody you love.

It doesn't feel cold when he removes my clothes. I only feel the warmth that comes off him when he presses up against me . . I only feel the warmth we make when we are siamese . . and I don't feel the pain anymore . . I only feel him inside me . . safe and warm and I know then that no matter what happens I will be okay . . that it's okay to be me . . because sometimes it's perfect to be me.

My mother is waiting for me when I come in.

It's late and Malky is already in bed. My mother is up watching the television with the sound off. Her eyes are red. I can tell the time by how sore they are.

I didn't mean to make her worry . . I didn't mean to be late. It was like time didn't exist anymore when I was with him. It stood still while we looked into each other's eyes until it got too dark to see . . until it was time to leave and we walked the whole way to the bus station.

It wasn't until the bus began to pull away . . his face pressed against the window and my hand waving to him that time started again . . and by that time it was already late.

I walked home.

I walked for three hours beside the road.

I could have called her but I needed to walk. I needed to be alone.

—I thought I'd lost you— she says when I come in the house . . rushes over to me . . hugs me the way she hasn't since I was younger.

I want to tell her I was already lost . . that I was lost for so long and only now she is finding me. I want to tell her that I'm okay now. I want to tell everything . . about Benji and Jenna and my dad. I want to say so much but nothing comes out.

But I don't have to tell her . . because she knows.

She is my mother and mothers always know.

She runs her hand through my hair . . lets me sob into her nightgown the way I used to . . whispers *—shhh shhh—* and says over and over again *—It's okay. Everything's going to be okay.—* and for the first time in a long time I believe her.

day 121

The envelope is sitting in my lap . . the top of it carefully torn open so that nothing is ruined. My name written on it . . perfectly straight letters.

It is only a photograph but I'm almost able to feel the way his hair used to feel. Even without putting my fingers in my mouth I can remember the way it felt when we kissed . . each and every time we kissed.

I reach for my stuffed raccoon . . the one I've named after him . . the one that smells the way his clothes used to smell . . the stale scent of dust and sunbeams.

Gretchen is reading the letter. I've already read it three times since I came back into the bedroom . . since my mom called me down to tell me it was here. I have it mem-

orized . . the words . . the little lines that make up each letter like the lines in a drawing that is so beautiful you can't
look at it too long.

It says he's happier.
It says he misses me.

He tells me about his dad and his dad seems like a nice
person. He tells me they get along and I'm happy for him.
He tells me how he looks for me all the time in the crowds
of people and that makes me smile.

Gretchen puts the pages down . . looks at me and we
both smile. I don't have to worry about saying the wrong
thing with her . . I don't have to say anything if I don't want
to because she understands what it means to lose people
and how it feels when you find them again even if it's only
in words that are written down on two folded pieces of
paper.

But the best part is that I'm not afraid to say what I want
to her . . I'm not worried about her telling someone else or
thinking I'm gay when I hold her hand. And I don't have to
worry about being alone because I have her . . I have my
best friend.

I lie down on the bed . . my head resting on her knees . . my black curly hair like nighttime against her pale skin.

I listen to the birds outside my window . . tired from flying back for the spring.

I listen to the leaves rustle in the wind . . the light coming through my window tinted green as it filters through the leaves. I wait before I speak . . wait to listen for a little while before we begin to whisper to each other . . before we share our secrets and tell each other our dreams.

She will tell me about the park in the city where she used to watch the sun rise and I will tell her about the house in the woods where I used to watch it set. She will tell me more about the girl before me . . the girl with black hair like mine. I will tell her about the boy that has blond hair like hers and we'll both begin to feel better by talking.

But before we say anything today I want to listen to the birds sing . . I want to close my eyes and pretend I am flying with them . . flying above our house where my brother is playing with my mom in the backyard with trees planted exactly three feet apart . . their laughter getting quieter as I fly farther.

And if I keep my eyes closed tight enough I can pretend to see me lying in the window . . getting smaller as I fly higher into the clouds that are waiting to catch me. I can see Gretchen with her fingers running through my hair and whispering things to me that make me laugh.

And just before I can see the castle on the clouds I can look down one last time and see the world so far below me.

A pretty world. A perfect one.